SCOOP McLAREN

· DETECTIVE EDITOR ·

Helen Castles

PROLOGUE

It appeared at exactly one minute past midnight.

I woke up to the summer sun streaming in on my face and the sound of my alarm. Turning back the covers, I rolled over and sleepily felt around my bedside table.

I was in one of those states where you're not asleep but not quite awake either, leaving you a bit confused as to whether what's happening is actually real or just your mind playing silly tricks on you.

Grabbing hold of my phone and squinting, I stared at the screen. Unfortunately for me, and every other resident in our little seaside paradise, the message was real, in fact it was about as real as it could possibly get.

It was from Evie.

Have you heard? Look outside!

I climbed out of my bed and stumbled across the floor to the window, still rubbing sleep from my eyes. I peered out.

Alligators! Big, ugly, scaly, scary alligators... everywhere!

Gasping, I jumped back from the window, tripping on my backpack and landing square on my bottom.

Oh... fudge!

Suddenly I was wide awake.

Rushing back to my phone, I quickly typed:

What's going on? Why is there a giant alligator in my back yard?

Go to your Inbox. It's the worst news ever!

I clicked on my email, and there it was.

It seemed to be an online newspaper, not unlike my own, but the headline was horrifying.

HIGGITY HARBOUR OVERRUN BY ALLIGATORS

It was a mass confusion and outright mayhem on the otherwise peaceful streets of the town of Higgity

Harbour. People had to climb trees, lock themselves in their cars, settle on their rooftops, anything to get away from the ferocious beasts!

Heart pounding, I read on.

It said the alligators would disappear, just on sunset (*phew!*), but to stay tuned for another edition tomorrow. It promised more terrifying events and claimed that it was the only newspaper to deliver the news *before* it happened.

I'm usually pretty calm and rational, and I would normally have said, 'This is impossible!' but...

Tap, tap, tap!

...there was an alligator, tapping its tail at my bedroom window, that made me think otherwise.

It appeared at exactly one minute past midnight.

The Dark Times.

CHAPTER ONE

TOWN JUMPING MAD AFTER DOWNPOUR OF FROGS

By Scoop Mclaren

The residents of Higgity Harbour were sent into a frenzy today when over 10,000 frogs mysteriously rained from the heavens.

Outdoor work was rendered impossible, while roads had to be closed in the interests of driver safety as the slithery amphibians fell from every direction and took over the town.

Frogs have been found in mail boxes, chicken coops, lawnmowers and, in numerous cases, the creatures have made their way inside houses and were even found in shoes!

Main Street resident, Iris Lumgarten, who professes to having a deep-seated fear of frogs, told *Click!* that she even found a frog in her underwear drawer.

'There I was, grabbing a fresh pair of underwear when all of a sudden the thing lunged at me,' she said.

'It was the worst experience of my life and I'm not exaggerating. I never, never, ever, ever exaggerate. Not ever!'

Shops were closed and a curfew was imposed on the town as experts warned that once a frog has gotten itself tangled in a human's hair, it could take hours, even days, to free the sticky amphibian.

Council ranger, Larry Perkins, tasked with eradicating the situation, quit his job in the middle of the saga.

'The infestation is too great,' Mr Perkins said. 'There's nothing I can do!'

Local police are also powerless to help, with Sergeant Mick Andrews unable to be awakened due to a strange condition. Doctors suspect it has something to do with the fact that he was bitten by a mean-looking bullfrog while trying to catch it.

The downpour steadied at around noon and the curfew was lifted a couple of hours later; however, residents are expected to be seeing, and finding, frogs for some time to come.

It rained frogs today.

Oh, we all knew it was going to happen, but even so nothing ever really prepares you for a day in which it pours frogs.

Our neighbour Mrs Bailey got one stuck in her hair on the way to collecting her mail. She had the misfortune of coming across a particularly angry little fellow. I heard her tell Dad that this was it – from now on, if anything other than rain was predicted to fall from the sky, she would securely lock her door, climb under her bed and not venture out again until the day was over.

Dad calls Mrs Bailey 'old misery guts' and said he wishes it would rain frogs every day so he wouldn't have to see her!

How did we know it was going to rain frogs? Well, it's quite a long story, but I'll give you the shortest version possible.

Firstly, and probably most importantly, my name is Henley McLaren but everyone calls me Scoop because I am the editor of my own online newspaper. Everyone except my dad that is. He's the *real* newspaper editor in our town.

Dad writes the *Higgity Harbour Gazette*, twice a week (Mondays and Thursdays), and has Kenny

Dixon (he's in year 10) deliver it. It has a circulation (that's how many copies are put out) of 900, and despite my insistence, he has no digital presence.

My online paper is called *Click!* I upload it daily and just yesterday it was shared 756 times. That's right, you read correctly – 756 times. In one day. Pretty impressive if you ask me, which everyone does, because I'm the girl people turn to when they need help. You see, I solve mysteries and, apart from being extremely good at it, I guess that's just what a proper detective editor does.

For instance, I solved an incredibly tricky mystery just last month that even had Sergeant Andrews baffled!

The people of Higgity Harbour had been reporting seeing strange lights in the night sky. I don't really believe in UFOs (if I were to see an alien, face to face, I might change my mind), so I just knew that there had to be another explanation. And I was right, because there was.

After launching my investigation, I managed to get clearance from a nearby air force base to talk to personnel. Even my dad has never been able to do that! After an interview with an air force major, I ruled out military drones. Then I had a better idea.

I knew we were close to an airport and, after making a few phone calls, I realised the lights were coming from regular aircraft that were waiting for a space on the runway for them to land. According to my sources, it didn't happen very often as planes have a precise landing schedule.

Mystery solved!

I'm mostly known around Higgity Harbour for my inquisitive (nosy) nature, which I get from my dad. I certainly don't get it from my mum. She lives in Spain and is a dog trainer.

I'm also known for my sparkly silver pen that Dad gave me on my tenth birthday and I rarely go anywhere without it. Dad says it's magic because it never runs out of ink, but Mum said Dad replaces the ink cartridge every three months, without me knowing.

Along with my sparkly pen, I carry a small notebook, wherever I go, in case there's a story and I need to take notes. Don't get me wrong, I rely on modern technology just as much as the next journalist, but my trusty pen and notebook are my backup. Technology can (and does!) go wrong, while a notebook can *never* run out of battery.

When I was a little girl (I'm thirteen now), Dad

used to take me everywhere to get the news and I learned a lot. Dad always says, 'The news never sleeps' and he's right. But lately, about the past year I'd say, or since I've been writing my own newspaper, Dad's not so keen to have me tag along any more. He says I'm getting in the way and that I ask too many questions. I say he's taught me well.

My best friend Evie Andrews is my roving reporter on the ground and together we make a great team. Sergeant Andrews is her dad.

Evie is feisty, pushy, outspoken and overconfident. All the traits you need to be a successful reporter. She once got an exclusive with Clive Edwards – Higgity Harbour's best gardener – after his 200lb pumpkin made it into the *Guinness Book of Records*. He's very shy and refused to speak to any local press, but Evie refused to take no for an answer. She sat on his front steps singing 'Three Blind Mice' for four hours straight until Mr Edwards couldn't take it any more. That was our best front page that week, complete with a picture of Mr Edwards with his humongous pumpkin.

Evie is also a brown belt in karate, just two belts away from becoming a master! She's a Girl Scout too. Both of these pastimes make her one of the most clever people to have around.

Getting news around Higgity Harbour has never been easy, however. It's not the most interesting town on the planet.

Higgity Harbour is a pretty little seaside town where everybody knows everybody and life is peaceful.

In the town square is a big, brass, life-size statue of Henry Higgity, a merchant sailor who discovered our little cove. Legend has it that Henry docked in the harbour at precisely the same time as infamous pirate Deadeye Dan Durnam. Deadeye Dan challenged Henry to a duel at the exact location where the town square now stands, the winner of which could claim the discovery. Henry beat Deadeye Dan (apparently he poked out his eye!) and then vowed never to leave Higgity Harbour's glorious shores.

They are both buried in the old cemetery near Doctor Blaxland's house, and according to the legend, whoever looks at Deadeye Dan's grave at the stroke of midnight turns to dust! I don't really believe in *that* part of the legend but, just to be sure, I stay well away from the old cemetery!

Higgity Harbour's main street is lined with cherry blossoms that bloom in a dazzling display of pink every spring. We even have The Cherry Blossom Festival each April where kids bob for apples, get sick on fairy floss and Miss Cherry Blossom is crowned.

Visitors also flock to the harbour in the summer when the population almost doubles, mostly with keen surfers taking advantage of our five-mile beach which some call 'surfer's paradise'.

Although it's usually a quiet little cove, over the past couple of months we've been experiencing interesting happenings in Higgity Harbour – not to mention peculiar – on a daily basis, and it's all because of a mysterious daily online newspaper, *The Dark Times*, and its mean editor, Sonny Fink.

Nobody knows who Sonny Fink is, and the newspaper magically appears in everybody's email inbox at exactly one minute after midnight. Whatever is written in the paper happens that very day, but the trouble is, it's always, *always* bad news.

That's how we knew that today it would rain frogs: it was in *The Dark Times*. And yesterday the mail truck got stuck in a snow storm (in the middle of summer!), leaving townspeople with no mail. Last week the supermarket burned to the ground in the middle of the night, and then the next day there was a sixteen-hour blackout that melted all the delicious treats at Mr Langton's ice creamery.

Exactly *how* Sonny Fink makes the news happen,

nobody knows. And *why*, well that's another mystery. All we know for sure is that this Sonny Fink is a real piece of work and is ruining the lives of everyone in Higgity Harbour. Six families have already had enough: they've packed up and moved! And quite apart from the horrible effect these happenings are having on our town, people have been reading Sonny's newspaper over mine and my dad's. We've been ditched! Dad's readership has dropped down to 600 and, last week, 170 readers abandoned my online paper in favour of Sonny's.

Sonny Fink's power is unbelievable and no one knows what will happen next.

♥

Evie and I met at the library at four o'clock to discuss the situation. We're currently on summer holidays so that leaves us plenty of free time to solve this mystery.

Our usual hangout was Mr Langton's ice creamery, but we all know what happened there.

By the time four o'clock rolled around, it had stopped raining frogs, but I sure came across a few on the way.

'So I scheduled an appointment and spoke with

Mayor Ludwick this morning,' Evie said, as we sat in the preschool corner (it has heaps of comfy cushions!), dodging glares from the cranky librarian, Esther Jennings. She knew we were only there because the ice creamery melted.

'Well, what did he say?'

'Get this – he thinks the townspeople should just focus all their energies on simply *dealing* with the daily dilemmas and that at least we *know* what's ahead of us. He said, "Forewarned is forearmed, Evie." Can you believe that? He's not even trying. And he calls himself the Mayor!'

'Good work,' I told her with a wink. 'And there's your angle – the one person who is supposed to lead our town through a crisis, and he couldn't care less. Headline: *Mayor refuses to take a stand on Fink.*'

'Nice one.'

'The Mayor might not be worried but I am. My dad and I have competition. Nobody's going to read our newspapers when they can get the news before it even happens. If we don't find out exactly who Sonny Fink is, we're done for.'

'So can we enlist the help of your dad then?'

'Afraid not. I've never seen him so out of sorts... I think he's given up. He told me last night he may as well quit the paper and go and live on a houseboat.'

'You want to live on a houseboat?' Evie asked.

'Not with my fussy tummy,' I replied. 'It'd be Pukesville on a daily basis!'

'Well, I'd ask my dad to help but he's asleep thanks to that frog bite.' Evie was so angry she couldn't stop herself from saying it. Suddenly, she sat forward and blurted out: 'Oh, Sonny Fink, you are the worst person I've ever—'

'Shhhh!' Miss Jennings said, from behind her desk. Next thing, she was on her feet, finger pointed, lips pursed. 'If you two little *antigens* can't be quiet, you'll have to find somewhere else to sprawl,' she spat. 'And watch your backpack, Evie, it's about to fall.'

We looked over at Evie's backpack, sitting firmly on a chair.

'No, it's not going to—' but then it toppled over and fell with a thud. Evie shrugged.

I whipped out my phone (that Dad said I'm only supposed to use in emergencies) and googled 'antigen'. To be fair, in my line of work knowing the exact meaning of a word could actually be classed as an emergency.

I learned that 'antigen' is a toxin or other foreign substance that induces an immune response in the body. Now I don't really know what all that means, but it sounds bad.

'Jeez,' I told Evie as I read. 'That was a bit harsh.'

I looked over at her – she was frowning, her cheeks were aglow, her eyes all squinty and I just knew she was about to give Miss Jennings a right old serve back.

I calmed her down.

'Forget her,' I whispered. 'We are not toxins or other foreign substances that induce an immune response in the body.'

'No. We're nowhere near it!' she said.

'Ok, now, getting back to Fink. We're in agreement? The adults in this town aren't doing anything to help the situation, so it's up to us now.'

'Absolutely. I'm so disappointed in the lot of them, and when this is all over I'm going to write a strongly worded opinion piece telling them so... With your permission, of course, boss,' she added.

I nodded. 'Deal.'

We both sat up straight, locked pinky fingers and stared each other squarely in the eye. It's what we always do before we embark on a story that we know will blow the socks off the public and take a lot of hard work and dedication to cover. Like the time we had to prove it was Lenny Newman's dog, Stumpy, dumping his business on the newsagent's doorstep every morning. Lenny wasn't too pleased about the front page headline, but in the end the truth must always come out. It's our job to see to that.

'It's settled then,' Evie said, as we pinky-shook on it.

'Yes,' I told my friend. 'We are going to find out who Sonny Fink is. That mischief-making editor *will* be exposed.'

CHAPTER TWO

SUN MYSTERIOUSLY DISAPPEARS

By Scoop Mclaren

Higgity Harbour was shrouded in darkness today when the sun did not rise.

Residents went about their business as usual, but with a great degree of difficulty.

Milkman John Luck found himself right out of it when he ploughed into some tables outside Ivy Regan's café, breaking his leg in three places.

'I'm not used to delivering milk in the dark in the middle of summer,' he told *Click!* as paramedics lifted him into the back of an ambulance. 'I didn't see them, honestly I didn't. Now I'll be off work for months. I'm ruined!'

There was also considerable trouble across town when council workers lopped trees in Somerville Park.

May Franklin's morning walking group didn't see the work being carried out and with their headphones blaring in their ears, they didn't hear it either.

The group walked underneath a particularly overgrown oak tree, with 65-year-old Mrs Franklin taking a limb to the shoulder.

With the only ambulance in town tending to Mr Luck's broken leg, it was up to council workers to toss Mrs Franklin into the back of their work truck and drive her to the hospital.

Townsfolk waiting for the delivery of Ted McLaren's *Higgity Harbour Gazette* may be a little put out this afternoon, as paperboy Kenny Dixon makes his way around his route in the dark with nothing but his trusty push bike and a torch.

Kenny had just finished his paper run and it was my job to pay him and tally up the day's takings.

Dad's office is in a front room of our house. For the past thirty-five years, that's where he's written his paper.

'Thanks, Scoop,' Kenny said, as I handed him his money.

‘So tell me, how’d the paper run go in the dark today?’

‘Well, it took me twice as long but at least that corgi on Middleton Drive didn’t chase me.’ He grinned. ‘Can’t chase me if he can’t see me.’

‘Yeah, I suppose.’

He threw his paper-delivery bag on the floor (Dad really hates when he does that) and plonked himself down on Dad’s desk. Then he grabbed Dad’s spare laptop and fired it up. Kenny’s mother won’t let him have a computer at home. She says he’ll only use it to play games and I suspect she’s right.

‘Does your dad have solitaire on this?’ he asked.

‘No. Dad’s not into games, just work.’

He shrugged and shut the laptop down. ‘So, what’s news with you?’

I shook my head. Kenny of all people should know better.

‘I can’t tell you that, Kenny. You know the rules.’

‘I know, I know. If you tell me now, I won’t read the paper.’

‘Exactly.’

He looked around the office. For a boy mostly just interested in sport there wouldn’t really be much in a news room that’d hold his attention for very long.

A few seconds later, and he was back to annoying me.

'You just going to sit around here until your dad comes home? Because a bunch of us is going down to the basketball courts for a game or two. Wanna come?' he asked.

'In the dark?'

'Why not? It'll be fun.'

'Not really my idea of fun. Besides, I really should get started on the next paper.'

I counted up the last of the day's takings and shoved it in Dad's top drawer.

Kenny shrugged. 'Jeez, you're boring sometimes, Scoop. It's the summer holidays. Can't you just chill out with us for a while?'

'I can't, Kenny, because the news—'

'Never sleeps. Or in this case, never takes a holiday. I know!' He rolled his eyes.

It really annoyed me when he did that.

'Mayor Ludwick isn't interested in finding out who Sonny Fink is, but Evie and I are. We're on the case.'

'Mayor Ludwick? Sonny Fink? Bo-ring again! You know, you really should come to bubble football on Saturday. Starts at ten at the football pitches.'

'That's a great idea,' I told him. 'I'll take my camera,

do a pics page for my newspaper. Thanks, Kenny.'

'No, *you* should come. Henley McLaren. Leave Scoop McLaren and your camera at home. Have some fun for once.'

He jumped up from Dad's desk and was halfway out of the door before I could come up with my reply.

'What I do *is* fun,' I said, but I don't think Kenny heard me. Even if he did hear me, I don't think he'd believe me.

He met Dad in the hallway just as he arrived home.

'Hiya, Mr M.'

'Hello, Kenny. How'd the paper run go in the dark?' Dad asked him.

'Not too bad. I can handle whatever Sonny Fink throws at me.'

Dad laughed and roughed up Kenny's hair.

'That's my boy,' he said.

'Anyway, see ya.'

I couldn't wait to tell Dad about Mayor Ludwick and the injustice of it all. He used to *live* for stories like this, and I was keen to get his mind off houseboats and interested in the news again.

I found him in the kitchen tasting my spaghetti sauce that I had simmering for dinner.

'Any good?' I asked, plonking down on a stool.

'Hmmm, lovely. You're becoming quite the master chef,' he said, as he kissed my forehead. 'How was your day?'

'Dark,' I replied.

'Yeah. I did notice that.'

'Dad, Evie and I have been thinking and we've come up with a great idea. It's going to lead to the scoop of the decade.'

Instead of being interested, Dad just laughed.

'What is it? Have you finally uncovered who swiped Mrs Tingle's mail box?'

'No, I'm still working on that one. I'm more interested in exposing Sonny Fink.'

Dad's smile faded. Talking about Sonny Fink stressed him out. I knew, because Mum always said that when Dad was stressed, he wore his shoulders for earrings. And now there he was, his shoulders up to his ears.

He sat down on the kitchen stool next to me. I'd hoped he'd be excited, maybe even a little proud that his daughter was taking on such a big story, but he simply said: 'Oh, that.'

'That? *That?* Dad, Sonny Fink is ruining the town, not to mention our newspapers. Things are going from bad to worse around here, and nobody, apart from Evie and I, even seems to care!'

'That's because, dear daughter, readers only care about three things – the state of their roads, how much rates they have to pay and if their rubbish is going to be collected. As long as the local council keeps these three things in check, people don't really worry about much else that goes on around here. Oh, and sport. They *love* sport,' he said.

A few years ago, a story like Sonny Fink would have my dad up all night, typing away, trying to get the story out before the bigger, city newspapers got a hold of it. Nowadays, all he cares about is council news. He gets out-scooped, on an almost weekly basis, and he doesn't even care.

'But you once told me that the best stories often come from the most unexpected places, the places closest to people's hearts.' I spun around to the kitchen counter and flipped open my laptop. 'Exposing Sonny Fink sounds *way* more interesting to me, and in tomorrow's paper there's a story all about Mayor Ludwick and how he's doing absolutely nothing to help the town he's meant to be in charge of.'

Dad's face flushed pink and I could clearly hear the anger in his voice.

'Oh, no, there won't be,' he protested. 'Kevin

Ludwick is a friend of mine.'

'You can't let mates stand in the way of the truth, Dad.'

'Now you look here, Henley Sarah McLaren.'

Oh boy, full name. I'm in big trouble.

'I don't want you to go making trouble where there is none,' Dad said. 'I'd expect that from *The Dark Times*, but I won't tolerate it from my own daughter. Anything you write in that… newspaper of yours, I want to read before print.'

'Before upload.'

'Whatever! I want to see it first.'

'But, Dad, you always taught me—'

'That's the end of this conversation, Henley.'

He got up, turned his back on me and started stirring the heck out of the spaghetti sauce. Suddenly I didn't feel hungry any more.

'Everyone calls me Scoop,' I said between my teeth, as I packed up my laptop and headed to my room.

♥

I was setting up my desk, getting ready to put tomorrow's paper together when I heard a familiar *ding* from my computer. It was Evie on messenger.

Hey DE!

Evie and I have a secret greeting we use when texting or messaging. She calls me DE (Detective Editor) and I call her RR (Roving Reporter). We think it's pretty cool. Someday, when we're not busy solving a mystery, we plan to come up with our very own secret language. How cool would *that* be?

I sat down and started typing.

Hiya RR!

I've almost finished my story on Mayor Ludwick. :)

Amazing! You never miss a deadline! When you're finished, send it through. I'll go over it (although I'm sure it's perfect!) and I can start putting tomorrow's paper together.

I don't think Mayor Ludwick is going to be very happy, but maybe this will be the push he needs to start taking Sonny Fink seriously?

Absolutely!

Mayor Ludwick wasn't the only person that would not be too pleased about tomorrow's issue of *Click!* My dad had made it very clear that I was to run every story past him before print and it's really not like me not to follow Dad's orders, but I just know I'm right about this. Sonny Fink must be stopped which means Evie and I must go ahead with the Mayor's story. I'll just have to answer to Dad later.

Still there, Scoop? Are you having second thoughts about uploading the story?

Hmm... No second thoughts, Evie! :) Ping me when you are done! YFIS, DE.

YFIS is our standard goodbye, and means Your Friend In Sleuthing.

Sure thing! YFIS, RR. :)

CHAPTER THREE

WORST FLOOD IN OVER A CENTURY

By Sonny Fink

Higgity Harbour residents will wake up today to the worst flood in 102 years. Declared as a state of natural disaster, Higgity Harbour will face repair bills in the millions.

The water will be gone by midday, but it could be days before the full extent of the damage is known.

Main Street businesses will bear the full force of the flood, with only the first-floor residences spared.

The flood could not come at a worse time for the town's golf enthusiasts, with their annual Higgity Harbour Giddyup Golf tournament having to be cancelled due to the course being soaked to the core.

Five pivotal bridges will be washed away, and causeways, culverts and roads will all be damaged by the flood.

More rain is predicted to fall next week, which will result in more flooding.

Readers are reminded that *The Dark Times* is the only newspaper to deliver the news before it happens.

MAYOR REFUSES TO TAKE A STAND ON SONNY FINK

By Evie Andrews

The popularly elected mayor of Higgity Harbour, Kevin Ludwick, believes residents should not be concerned by the alarming turn of events lately, saying the editor of *The Dark Times*, Sonny Fink, is most likely here to stay and that residents should just deal with it.

Click! spoke to Mayor Ludwick in his council chambers where he was asked what he intends to do, as the man in charge of the town, about the increasing pandemonium inflicted upon Higgity Harbour thanks to the articles Sonny Fink writes.

'Well, when it comes to Sonny Fink and the... unpleasantness of the articles that Sonny writes, I think the townspeople should just focus all of their energies on simply dealing with the dilemmas. Forewarned is forearmed,' he said.

As Sonny Fink continues to rain madness upon Higgity Harbour, it seems nobody, not even the Mayor, is willing to step up and put an end to the bedlam!

Mayor Ludwick was not in a good mood. That's what I got told at the council's reception, anyway.

I was summoned to his office not long after our exclusive on him hit cyberspace, at precisely 12 noon.

I waited for the flood waters to recede, and at exactly twenty-three minutes after my paper was uploaded, I was sitting across from him at his desk in his office, which smelled oddly of mothballs and week-old apples.

He offered me a lollipop, like I was three, and frowned when I said I didn't want one.

'Now, Scoop, you and I need to have a little chat,' he said.

'Really?' I asked, playing dumb. 'Whatever for?'

'Now listen up, young lady. I've been speaking with your father, and I ask you… no, we *both* ask you to print a retraction in the very next issue of your newspaper.'

I blinked. (A retraction is something you write to take back something you've written before!) 'A retraction to say what?' I asked the Mayor.

'To say I'm not useless and incompetent, that's what!'

'But you are! And I only print the truth. Ugly as it may be.'

'But it isn't the truth!' he fired back. He swallowed hard. His eyes were bulging. I honestly thought his head was going to pop off. He got to his feet. 'You write one more word about me, and I'll see to it that that… measly little rag you call a newspaper never sees the light of day again! Do I make myself clear?'

It was right there and then that it dawned on me.

While Mayor Ludwick stared coldly at me with his piercing blue eyes, I realised who I might *actually* be dealing with. As I sat in that office, face to face with the Mayor, I felt a ball of energy whirling around in my stomach.

I was scared.

Maybe there was a very good reason *why* Mayor Ludwick wasn't doing a thing to catch Sonny Fink.

Maybe he *was* Sonny Fink...

I got up in shock and made my way towards the door.

'What are you doing? I'm not finished with you yet! What about that retraction?' he spat, looking furious. 'I want you to confirm you'll print that retraction!'

'I... I have to go,' I mumbled, running out.

♥

After my horrible meeting with the Mayor, I decided to go and sit in the town square.

It was a peaceful spot made up of lush green lawns and flower beds that, at this time of year, sprouted vibrant orange and yellow marigolds, teamed with red dahlias and dark blue daisies. I often came to the town square to think and, today, I had a lot to think about.

On the other side of the square Miss Jennings sat on a bench, eating a sandwich with a thermos of tea next to her. She took lunch in the town square every day at 1 p.m. You could set your watch by it.

I waited for her to look in my direction and when she did I gave her a wave. I think she pretended not to notice as she looked in the opposite direction.

Typical.

To be perfectly honest, I really hoped I would come across a friendly face. My encounter with the Mayor had left me a little shaky. I don't like being yelled at and besides that, if he really is Sonny Fink, maybe his next headline will now be about me?

I wondered what sort of things he could do to me in *The Dark Times*. Turn me blue? Make all my long strawberry blonde hair fall out? My tongue disappear so that I can't ask questions any more or make my hands fall off so I can't write? *Grow devil horns on my head?* The (horrible) list was endless!

I sat down at the foot of the Henry Higgity statue and looked up at him, our town hero. He looked so brave and wise, staring out towards the ocean with hands on his hips and purpose in his eyes. We learned all about Henry Higgity in history class.

It was Henry who started the harbour's very first newspaper. And he was our first Mayor. He also gave money to build the first hospital and founded the Higgity Harbour Life Saving Club. His love for the harbour was clearly evident in history books, and a wave of sadness swept over me as I imagined what he would think about the dark cloud we now found ourselves under, courtesy of Sonny Fink.

'What would you do, Henry?' I asked.

'I'd give up… if I were you,' a voice replied.

Then Imogen Blaxland stepped out from behind the statue. She was carrying her hot pink laptop with a fashionable handbag to match.

I blushed. *Caught talking to a statue!*

Imogen Blaxland is the most wicked girl at school, possibly the most wicked girl on the planet. She's in my class, all the teachers are scared of her, she has no friends and that's just the way she seems to like it. Her dad, Doctor Blaxland, is so nice. I don't know where she gets her nastiness from.

'Oh, it's you,' I said. 'What are you doing here? Why are you hiding?'

'Taken to interviewing statues now, have you?' she asked me, ignoring *my* questions. 'Sounds like Higgity Harbour's very own mystery solving detective editor is all out of leads? What a shame.'

She sat down next to me and opened her laptop.

'I'm not *all* out of leads, Imogen. I'm just…'

'All out of leads?'

'Thinking. I'm just thinking. That's all,' I said as I carefully helped a baby ladybug that had found its way onto my arm, down to the lawn.

She rolled her eyes and started typing. I leaned over to get a peek at her work but she turned herself and her laptop away from me.

'What are you writing?' I asked. 'I didn't know you were interested in writing. You've never showed any interest at school.'

'It's none of your business,' she said, squinting her eyes at me. 'You stick to *your* online newspaper… and I'll stick to *mine*.'

I sprung up. 'You don't have an online newspaper!'

'Don't I?' she smiled, and not in a nice way.

'What are you up to?' I asked, folding my arms.

'You're the know-it-all detective – you tell me.'

Oh… bum! She is soooooo annoying!

'I thought you were going to London for the summer holidays, with your mum?' I asked her.

She looked up at me, brushing a black curl from her forehead. She had frizzy, what looked like *totally* uncontrollable hair and a face full of brown freckles.

'I decided that I couldn't be bothered visiting Big Ben and taking tea with the Queen,' she chimed, pulling her laptop closer.

'You can't just take tea with the Queen anytime you feel like it, Imogen. That's not how it works.'

'You can when you're related to Her Majesty,' she spat.

I sat back down next to her, stretching my legs out and folding my arms behind my head. 'That's a loose truth and you know it. Just because your mother's great, great, great grandmother's second cousin was a lady in waiting, does *not* make you related to the Queen.'

'Whatever.'

She started typing again, every now and then stealing a look at me out of the corner of her eye to see if I was watching.

'What's your newspaper called?' I asked.

'It's called the *None of Your Business Tribune*,' she quipped, 'and it's *way* better than your silly *Click!* That much I *can* tell you.'

I didn't let it get to me. I knew that Imogen Blaxland was, in actual fact, an avid reader of *Click!* Her dad told me so. The day I had an ear infection and Dad took me to Doctor Blaxland's surgery. Her dad told me that she reads every issue, back to front and then over again. He also told me that she wished *she* could have her own newspaper. Nevertheless, I didn't let on to Imogen.

'Are you trying to find out who Sonny Fink is as well?' I asked her. 'Is that what you're writing about?'

She stared at me and laughed. 'Why on earth would I be doing that? I think Sonny Fink is truly the best newspaper editor in the whole entire world. I hope Sonny Fink is *never* caught.'

Well, this is a first. Sonny Fink has a fan!

'Are you daft?' I cried, facing her. 'Sonny Fink is ruining Higgity Harbour, day by day! Why in the world would you want the mayhem to continue?'

She turned and looked at me, her face lit up like a Christmas tree.

'Why in the world would you want to stop it?' she grinned. 'Frogs raining from the heavens? Darkness all day long? Floods? Who knows what will happen next? It's so… so… exciting and… beguiling! I think Sonny Fink is the best thing that is happening to this town since… since…'

Suddenly her face fell and she frowned. 'I… I don't want to talk about it any more. I've said too much already,' she said. She turned away and began madly typing again.

'Fine by me,' I shrugged. 'I just came here to enjoy the sunshine and the flowers and the pretty periwinkles singing, anyway.'

She huffed. 'Periwinkles. *Yuck!*'

We sat in an awkward silence for a little while with Imogen only stopping her typing to give me a death stare every minute or so.

'What's your readership?' I asked.

'What?'

'Your readership? What is it?'

She looked at me blankly. 'It… it doesn't *need* a readership, Scoop.'

'A readership is an estimation of how many people read it, so, yes, Imogen, you definitely *need* a readership,' I smiled.

I could've laughed but Dad says it's never polite to make someone feel stupid. I think she felt stupid anyway.

She slammed her laptop shut, tucked it under her arm and rose to her feet. Swinging her hot pink handbag over her left shoulder, she snarled, 'You think you're *so* clever.'

'No I don't. I'm just telling you that—'

'Well here's a newsflash for you, Scoop McLaren. By the time Sonny Fink is finished with Higgity Harbour, you won't have a readership left!'

CHAPTER FOUR

I sat in Mr Mack's café on the beach, sipping on a vanilla milkshake and messaging Evie to tell her all about my encounter with Imogen.

Mr Mack was once a professional surfer. Dad said he was pretty good too, but that was years ago. Now he runs a little café on the shore, that is also a surf shack, where surfers go to get their boards waxed and kids hang out for the cheap milkshakes and the free surf tips. *When* Mr Mack's in a good mood, that is. Which is hardly ever.

Mr Mack has long, silver-grey hair which he wears in a ponytail. Sometimes he even plaits it. He's always wearing colourful board shorts and loud Hawaiian shirts, which seems peculiar to me because his clothes definitely do *not* match his watery personality.

Despite Mr Mack being a bit of a cranky pants, the surf shack is usually a fun place to hang out. Apart from being right on the beach, it has seriously comfy lime green booths that you can sink right into and funky surfboards hang from the ceiling. There are pictures of Mr Mack surfing when he was younger, all over the walls.

Evie replied.

Imogen Blaxland is just trying to get under your skin, Scoop. Don't let her get to you. She's not up to anything and she doesn't have her own online newspaper. She just likes torturing people, it's part of her... VIP. Euh... DNA.

Right. It's in her blood. I guess you're right. Besides, we have bigger things to think about – like catching Sonny Fink! Still ok to meet me at the library in the morning?

Sure thing. 9 a.m. sharp?

Yes. We'll put our heads together and compile a list of suspects so get thinking, ok?

Ok, boss. YFIS, RR.

I'll do the same. See you there. YFIS, DE. :)

I flipped open my laptop, started up a new Word document and typed SUSPECTS at the top of the page. Then underneath I wrote:

SUSPECT NUMBER ONE: Mayor Kevin Ludwick. MOTIVE: Currently unknown. PROOF: Not doing a thing to help catch Sonny Fink even though, as the Mayor, he is in charge of the town's wellbeing.

Downing the last of my milkshake, I thought long and hard before I took to the keyboard again.

I stared out at the ocean, watching the waves crash on the shore and replaying the conversation I had with Imogen in the town square over and over again in my mind.

Finally I wrote:

SUSPECT NUMBER TWO: Imogen Blaxland. MOTIVE: Likes the excitement and hates me with a passion! PROOF: Openly admits to being a fan of Fink's and claims to have an online newspaper.

Is Imogen clever enough to be Sonny Fink? I know she's nasty enough, but an evil newspaper editor?

I decided that Evie was right. Imogen was just trying to push my buttons. She did it at school all the time. I highlighted her name, motive and proof, and then pressed DELETE. That left me with one solid suspect: the Mayor.

I was just about to pack up my laptop when Mr Mack walked over with a worn-out old cloth in his hand. He looked down at me and sighed.

'You have been sitting in here, chatting away on that computer for exactly *two* hours and you have bought exactly *one* milkshake,' he said, wiping down the table around my laptop. 'I'm not running a social club here, Scoop McLaren. Either you buy something else or you hit the road.'

'Sorry, Mr Mack,' I said, handing him my empty glass. 'That was the last of my allowance for the week.'

'Then I guess I'll be having the privilege of your oh-so-generous patronage some other day,' he frowned. 'Goodbye.'

♥

On my way home, it was almost dark when I walked past the council chambers car park. There were only two cars left – Miss Morrison from account's red Mini and Mayor Ludwick's town car.

I didn't plan on stopping but when I saw Mayor Ludwick waltz out of the council building, swinging his briefcase, talking on his phone and shaking his fist, I decided to do a little investigating. Perhaps I could pick up a clue? Either one that would clear Mayor Ludwick of being Sonny Fink, or point the finger straight at him.

I quickly ducked behind Miss Morrison's Mini and listened intently.

'She was in my office today, flaunting that newspaper of hers in my face, refusing to print a retraction,' he spat. 'That child is getting on my last nerve!'

Me! He was talking about me!

'If she comes near me again, if she writes one more word about me in that blasted newspaper of hers, I'm going to the press council to make a formal complaint. She's on some… vigilante… power trip, hounding me. She's hounding me I tell you. It's tantamount to harassment!'

Mental note: google 'vigilante' and 'tantamount.'

Just then, I spied Miss Morrison, flinging the council doors open and walking towards her car. 'Night, Mayor Ludwick,' she said, giving him a wave.

'What? Oh, yes, goodnight,' he mumbled, turning his back on her and continuing on the phone.

Oh no, I have to move. And Mayor Ludwick's car is the only one left!

I kept down low and waddled my way over to the

Mayor's car. I was getting closer to him, so close I could hear him panting with anger, his chubby little chest heaving up and down like a bullfrog.

Miss Morrison got into her Mini and drove off, tooting her horn behind her.

'What? Of course I don't think she knows anything,' Mayor Ludwick continued. 'How could she possibly know anything? But if she keeps digging…' he breathed in hard, like he was about to explode. 'I would just rather be kept out of the spotlight at a time like this, if you know what I mean.'

A time like what?

'That little girl… detective… newspaper... whatever has gone too far this time, and if that father of hers won't stop her, *I* will!'

Yikes!

He hung up, threw his phone into his briefcase and marched towards his car. *Towards me!*

I bobbed down even further, as far as I could go. The only way I could gauge his location was to watch his little feet under the car.

I was on the other side, near the back tyre, hunched down and praying that, once he started the engine, I could quickly make it to the side of the council chambers and out of sight, without him seeing me.

I held my breath as I watched his feet at the driver's side door.

That's it, I silently urged. *Just get in and drive off.*

Time seemed to stand still. I could feel my foot falling asleep but was powerless to give it a shake to wake it up. I turned sideways, just a little, hoping the slight movement would help but all it did was jolt my sparkly silver pen from my side jacket pocket. It hit the ground.

Flit!

Then it started to roll, right under the Mayor's car.

Suddenly he stopped.

Oh no! He heard my pen fall. Everyone in Higgity Harbour knows I own that pen. If he sees it, it'll be the end of me!

His feet turned and he started walking toward the back of his car.

'Who's there?' he asked. 'Who's skulking around this government car park? I demand you show yourself. SHOW YOURSELF NOWWWWW!'

Oh no! This is it! I'm a goner!

I thought about running. Maybe with the fast approaching darkness, he wouldn't realise that it was me? Just a shadowy non descript figure, no proof at all that it was *Click!'s* Scoop McLaren. But I needed to get my pen. Apart from the fact that it's probably my most prized possession and a special gift from my dad, if I leave it behind, it's sure-fire proof that I was here, following the Mayor. Eavesdropping. Hounding him! He'd take it to the press council for certain!

Darn foot. WAKE UP!

I leaned down to get a location on my pen, under the car, and I saw him stop. His feet turned again.

'Is anybody here?' he asked. 'As Mayor of Higgity Harbour I demand that you show yourself!'

I watched as his stumpy little feet turned and took off towards the back of the car again. A few more steps, around the trunk, and he'd see me!

Just run for it, Scoop, I told myself. *JUST RUN!*

Then something wonderful happened. I heard: '*London Bridge is falling down, falling down, falling down…*' It was his phone ringing.

I saw his feet stop and I listened as he felt around his briefcase for his phone.

London Bridge is falling—

'Yes, hello, what?' he answered. 'Is that *really* an official mayoral duty? At this time of the evening?'

Yes! Yes, it is!

'Well can't it wait until the council meeting tonight?'

No, no it can't. JUST GO!

'All right. I'm on my way.'

Phew!

He walked back towards the driver's side door, opened it up and got in. I felt the whir as he started the motor. Then I remembered.

Your pen, Scoop, YOUR PEN!

I closed my eyes, shoved my hand under the humming vehicle and grabbed for my precious pen.

Got it!

I pulled it from under the car just as the wheels started to roll and that's when I made my run for it. Still hunched down, I didn't look back, not until I was safely behind the council building.

Leaning against the cold brick wall, my heart was pounding so hard that I could feel it thumping in my ears. I carefully peeped around the corner and watched as Mayor Ludwick's tail lights faded off into the distance.

I whipped my phone out and googled 'vigilante'.

A self-appointed doer of justice.

CHAPTER FIVE

PATIENTS LEFT OUT IN THE STREET AS HOSPITAL DISAPPEARS

By Sonny Fink

In a strange turn of events, the Higgity Harbour District Hospital will disappear at exactly one minute past midnight, and patients and staff will be stranded on the street.

With nothing but a drip and a bedpan to his name, twelve-year-old patient Harry Davis will have to wait to have his tonsils out.

'It doesn't really worry me,' he will tell passers-by. 'Mum's making me have the operation. With any luck, the hospital will never come back!'

Head nurse Jill Gilles will not be at all happy about

the situation.

'I had a strawberry cheesecake and a chocolate doughnut in the fridge, and I was looking forward to devouring both when my shift ended. Now the fridge is gone,' she'll be heard to remark . 'This is a disaster!'

According to sources, the hospital will be back in its same location at midnight tonight; however, all records will have been permanently erased and head nurse Gilles' fridge will be empty.

Readers are reminded that *The Dark Times* is the only newspaper to deliver the news before it happens.

I didn't see Dad last night. He was late coming home from the council meeting and I was already in bed. By the way he slammed the kitchen cupboard doors this morning while he was making breakfast, I don't think he's too happy with me. I bet he saw Mayor Ludwick at the council meeting who told him about the no-retraction situation. *Darn!*

I snuck out of the back door and met Evie at the library at nine o'clock sharp to compile a list of suspects, and I knew exactly who would be top.

'Mayor Ludwick?' Evie asked. 'You think Sonny Fink is *Mayor Ludwick*?'

'Shhhh,' I told her. I could see Miss Jennings at her

desk, pretending to work, but I know eavesdropping when I see it.

'Sorry.' Evie lowered her voice. 'You think Sonny Fink is Mayor Ludwick?'

'Think about it. Maybe he's unwilling to expose Sonny Fink because he *is* Sonny Fink.'

'Makes sense,' Evie shrugged. 'But…'

'But what?'

'He doesn't seem too smart. I mean, to be a journo, you have to have some smartness about you. Mayor Ludwick always kind of struck me as a bit of a… dill.'

I shook my head. 'That's his cover, Evie. You need to learn to read people.'

Evie rolled her eyes at me.

'Plus, I was in the council car park last night and—'

'The council car park? *Last night?* What were you doing there?'

I shook my head again. 'Investigating, Evie, investigating!'

Her eyes widened. 'Got anything good?'

'Well I heard Mayor Ludwick on his phone saying how difficult I've been making his life lately.'

I looked up to see Miss Jennings had disappeared from her desk.

'So, Mayor Ludwick is your number-one suspect,

right?' Evie asked.

'Yep. Who's yours?'

Evie looked sheepish. She went red and squirmed in her seat as if she desperately didn't want to say what she was about to say.

'Well,' I said. 'Out with it.'

'I've been doing a lot of thinking about this... '

'I'd expect nothing less.'

'And I keep coming back to the same person. Time and time again.'

'Well? Who is it?'

'Well, it's kind of... sort of... your... dad,' she said.

'My dad?'

'Yep.'

'Ted McLaren?'

'Yep.'

I laughed out loud. It was lucky Miss Jennings wasn't at her desk or I'd have been rightly told off for making too much noise.

'What on earth makes you think it's my dad? He hates Sonny Fink as much as I do. He'd do anything to—'

Wait a second. Perhaps Evie had a point? Dad was just like Mayor Ludwick – he wasn't doing a thing to stop Sonny Fink, even though he probably has the most to lose by allowing Sonny a free rein. His paper has almost bitten the dust thanks to Sonny Fink. Maybe after all these years of staying up late to deliver the news (that never sleeps), Dad's finally lost it! Maybe it's easier for him to make the news, as Sonny Fink, than it is for him to actually go out and get it?

'Are you ok, Scoop?' Evie asked. 'I didn't mean to upset you. But he has changed – you said so yourself.'

I didn't respond. I had so many thoughts swirling around in my head.

For all the years Dad had been teaching me how to investigate a story, I never once thought that, one day, *he* would be the subject of my investigation.

'I'm sorry, Scoop,' Evie said. 'It's probably not your dad, but—'

'—but all avenues must be covered. Dad always says, you *must* report on the truth, no matter how ugly it may be,' I told my friend. 'And if Sonny Fink really is my dad, it won't get much uglier than that!'

♥

I had been home for about half an hour when Dad knocked on my bedroom door. I'd been avoiding him all afternoon for more reasons than one.

Firstly, I knew he was angry at me for uploading Evie's story about the Mayor. Secondly, I now had doubt in my mind. Doubt that the reason my dad had changed over the past couple of months had nothing to do with him being put out by Sonny Fink and everything to do with him *being* Sonny Fink.

Another thing also worried me. If he indeed was the editor of *The Dark Times*, maybe the popularity of *my* newspaper drove him to it?

I still couldn't discount Mayor Ludwick, though. These were the two strongest leads we had, and as a good detective editor, it was up to me to follow them through. *Both* of them.

'Come in,' I said.

Dad sat down on my desk chair, crossed his legs and sighed. Whenever we were about to have an uncomfortable conversation, he'd sit down on my desk chair, cross his legs and sigh. Like the time I needed a bra. I'm not even going to tell you how uncomfortable *that* conversation was...

Still, I'd take a million conversations about underwear over accusing my dad of being Sonny Fink.

'Young lady... '

'Yes, I know you're not happy with me, Dad, but today the hospital disappeared. It vanished, and sick people were left to roam the streets. Things are getting worse, and somebody has to be held accountable,' I said. I sat up on my bed and closed my laptop. Tomorrow's paper could wait.

'Don't get me wrong, Henley, I admire your tenacity—'

'Good,' I replied, making a mental note to later google 'tenacity'.

'But, as I've said to you before, there are rules when you're the head of a newspaper. Kevin Ludwick agreed to a conversation with Evie – off the record. He asked for his comments *not* to go into the paper, and you went ahead and did it anyway.'

'But, Dad—'

'No buts about it, Missy, you've forced my hand. I forbid you to write your paper for one whole week.'

'One whole week? Sonny Fink will have destroyed Higgity Harbour by then!'

'One whole week. And you will use that time to have a good, long think about the responsibility you have to the public. It's one thing to want to print the truth, but it's quite another to slander a council official.'

Dad got up to leave. That's when I blurted out: 'I think he's Sonny Fink, but... Evie thinks you are.'

He stopped dead in his tracks. He turned and looked at me in a way I've only seen my dad look once before. When Mum left.

'Do you think she's right?' he asked. 'Do *you* think I'm Sonny Fink?'

'I… I have to investigate every lead. I'm sorry, Dad.'

'I see,' he said. He turned and walked out, quietly closing my bedroom door behind him.

I grabbed my phone and googled 'tenacity'.

The quality or fact of being very determined.

Funny thing was, the quality Dad said he admired in me was the exact same thing I was now being punished for.

♥

I sneaked into my dad's room at one minute to midnight.

I couldn't sleep. I just had to know if my dad was Sonny Fink and, if he was, I had no idea what I was going to do about it.

We'd probably have to join Mum in Spain. I wondered if the police could extradite people from Spain. That'd never work, though. Mum and Dad don't get along much any more. Hence her address in Spain.

Besides, Dad would have to face his punishment, and I'd probably have to report on it in the newspaper, even though that would be the worst thing ever.

I felt sick.

I turned on my phone and waited (hopefully) for Sonny to upload the paper. Next thing the light came on. Dad sat upright in bed and fumbled for his glasses on the bedside table.

'Henley?' he asked as he put them on. 'Is that you? What are you doing up so late?'

I held my phone up. 'Googling "tenacity",' I told him.

He threw back the covers. 'Come on, jump in,' he said.

I slid into the bed and gave Dad a cuddle. It'd been a while since we cuddled. Ever since I started my paper.

'I know what you're doing,' he said, quietly. 'You're doing exactly what I would do in your shoes. You're waiting for Sonny Fink to upload the paper. Then you'll know it's not me.'

'I don't think it's you, Dad, honestly,' I told him. 'But you have been acting rather strange lately. And when Evie suggested it, I had to save face. I couldn't let her know that I wasn't willing to investigate you simply because you're my dad.'

'I know, I know,' he said. 'I've taught you well. You always do the right thing and have integrity. That's something you get from me.'

I looked at the clock. 'Dad, it's one minute past midnight.'

We watched the screen.

I'd never been so happy to see a Sonny Fink headline.

'It's out,' I sighed. 'You're not Sonny Fink. But, Dad, you know I—'

'You had to ask,' he said, as he patted my arm. 'I know. I have been… a bit out of it lately. I'm not Sonny Fink, though, sweetie. I'm just a bit tired.'

'I get it. Thirty-five years is a long time in the news. But that's what I'm for. I can help. If you'll let me. Maybe, someday, we'll join forces?'

'Perhaps. I'd like that.' He smiled. 'Someday.'

'In the meantime, how about you *un*forbid me—'

'That's not a word, Henley.'

'—from writing the paper and we join forces to catch Sonny Fink? Of course, Evie and I are perfectly capable of doing it on our own—'

'Oh, of course.'

'—but it would be nice to have someone with your

experience on the case.'

There was a pause. 'I don't know.'

'Please, Dad. You've taught me everything I know, and together, I don't think Sonny Fink stands a chance.'

Dad took a deep breath. 'Ok. I'll get on the phone first thing in the morning and speak to Kevin Ludwick. I'll suggest a meeting in his office. I'll ask Deputy Mayor Tom Willis to come along too – he's always been a sensible fellow.'

'Careful, Dad,' I warned. 'Kevin Ludwick is on the top of our very short list of suspects. In fact, now that you're in the clear, Ludwick is *the* suspect.'

CHAPTER SIX

MOUSE PLAGUE HITS CENTRAL COVE

By Sonny Fink

Higgity Harbour will be inundated with mice today.

Main Street resident, Iris Lumgarten, who has a deep-seated fear of frogs, will be absolutely livid.

'I'd prefer to be overrun by frogs any day,' she'll say. This morning, when Mrs Lumgarten will make breakfast, a cheeky little mouse will pop up out of her toaster! She will have to throw the thing away, along with all her shoes, her biscuit barrel, her rice, flour, sugar and cocoa – anything these horrible little creatures have touched, she will toss. She will be finding mice everywhere!

Mail will not be delivered after the feisty creatures eat through all the town's letters and parcels at the post office, while the fruit market will have to be closed due to there being more mice on the shelves than products.

Both of the town's banks will also have to be closed after mice will chew through wires, rendering computers useless and business impossible.

Residents will see the plague move on at sunset, but until then would be wise to watch their step.

Readers are reminded that *The Dark Times* is the only newspaper to deliver the news before it happens.

'My dad is definitely *not* Sonny Fink,' I told Evie, as we sat atop her mum's kitchen table.

With mice scurrying all over the kitchen floor, we had little choice. We soon found out, however, that mice can, in fact, climb up kitchen tables, and so spent half our time flicking the hairy little germ-traps off.

'At midnight last night I sneaked into his room and at exactly one minute past midnight Sonny Fink uploaded the story about the mouse plague. It was all the proof that I needed.'

'Well, that's a relief,' Evie said, stamping her feet and waving her arms around madly in a bid to scare the mice away. 'I'm really sorry I mentioned his name as a suspect, Scoop, but I just had a hunch. I guess my hunch was wrong.'

'We had to cover every base, Evie, so don't feel bad,' I told her. 'Besides, Dad's relieved to be in the clear, *and* he's agreed to help.'

'Awesome... *eekkk!*'

A rude little baby mouse ran right across her toes.

'I can handle snakes, I can handle spiders and I can handle alligators. I even handled the time Sonny Fink unleashed the swarm of bees, but I will not, I repeat, will *not* tolerate a mouse running across my toes!'

'I've got news for you and it's all bad,' I told her, as I stopped a mouse from running up my trouser leg. 'The mice are here until sunset. That's when Fink said the plague would go. Until then, we'll just have to keep shooing them away.'

'I really hate Sonny Fink,' Evie said, grabbing my arm for comfort.

'Don't worry,' I told her. 'With my dad on board, we're three times more powerful now. Sonny Fink doesn't stand a chance.'

♥

Word about our meeting with Mayor Ludwick had spread. When we got to the council chambers there was a big group of people waiting outside. I looked around at all the faces. I could see Iris Lumgarten; cranky Mrs Bailey from next door; milkman John Luck, hobbling on his crutches; and even Miss Jennings from the library.

I quickly checked my supplies – phone, notebook, sparkly pen and, most importantly, all the confidence I could muster. I was ready to take on the Mayor.

'Do you really think Mayor Ludwick could be Sonny Fink, Scoop?' Mrs Lumgarten asked me, as we made our way into the council chambers.

'We'll know more after the meeting,' I told her.

'All the best to you, Scoop,' John Luck said as he hobbled out of the way. 'If anyone can get it out of Ludwick, it's you.'

'Thank you, Mr Luck,' I replied. 'I'm super thankful for the vote of confidence!'

Waiting inside Mayor Ludwick's office, Deputy Mayor Tom Willis rested his hand on Dad's shoulder. He and my dad have been friends since for ever.

'We've really got to do something about this *Dark Times* newspaper, Ted,' Mr Willis said. 'I never did take this Fink character too seriously. Like everyone else, I thought the headlines added a bit of… excitement to the old place.'

Evie and I looked at each other and rolled our eyes.

Grown ups!

'But that mouse plague today did some real damage to my farm,' he continued, 'and with the sun disappearing the other day and then the flood, I can't have this maniac playing havoc with the weather, Ted. My farm will go under if Fink keeps this up!'

Dad nodded. 'We're all a bit guilty of being a *little* lax when it comes to Sonny Fink, Tom,' he said.

Evie and I looked at each other and rolled our eyes again. *Yeah, right!*

'But that's what this meeting is for,' Dad said.

'Can we count on your support, Mr Willis?' I leaned forward and asked.

'Until Fink is caught,' he said. Then he reached out and shook my hand.

'Thanks,' I smiled.

Mayor Ludwick sauntered in, ten minutes late. He didn't look too happy.

He positioned himself at his desk, shooing away a fluffy little mouse as it scurried across his computer keyboard.

I could hear that the townspeople, who by now had gathered outside the office door, were anxious to hear what was going on inside. These people had no idea who Sonny Fink was, and given what the rogue editor was capable of, they were understandably frightened.

'All right, let's get this meeting started,' Mayor Ludwick said. 'I don't have all day, you know. I'm a very busy and *extremely* important man.'

'Look, Kevin,' Mr Willis started. 'I've been your deputy for a long time now and while we haven't always seen eye to eye, I always thought I could trust you. But there have been some strange happenings in this town and you don't seem to be doing anything about it. Now, because of that, rumour has it that *you* may be Sonny Fink. Are you?'

Mayor Ludwick didn't say anything.

He just sat there, staring at us.

Evie stood up. 'Well? *Are* you?'

At that moment, Mayor Ludwick banged his fist down hard on his desk.

'I most certainly am *not* Sonny Fink,' he said. 'I may have been a tad… lazy in performing my mayoral duties of late, but I have nothing to do with that dreaded newspaper!'

I could hear the crowd outside becoming even more unsettled.

I looked over at Mayor Ludwick. He was all red-faced and sweating. I actually felt a bit sorry for him.

'All right,' I said. 'Everyone is innocent until proven guilty.'

'Well, you're the investigative reporter, Scoop,' Mr Willis said. 'Investigate him!'

Suddenly, Mayor Ludwick was on his feet. 'Now see here,' he said. 'I agreed to this meeting so that we could discuss what we're going to do about Sonny Fink, not to prove my innocence. I'm the town mayor for crying out loud! My innocence should go without saying!'

'We don't trust you, Ludwick,' someone called from outside. Then I heard 'Yeah!' as others shouted in agreement.

He's always been a bit strange!

I've never trusted him, his eyes are too beady!

Why isn't he helping to catch Fink?

Because he is Fink!

YEAH!

Then my dad stepped forward. He turned to Ludwick. 'Listen, Kevin, I don't think you're going to get out of here unless you can prove that you're not Sonny Fink.'

'But, but—'

'Mayor Ludwick, where were you at exactly one minute past midnight last night?' I asked.

'Speak louder,' a voice called from outside. 'We can't hear you! We want to know what's going on!'

'Mayor Ludwick? I'll ask you again,' I said, more loudly. 'Where were you at *one minute past midnight* last night? Can anyone confirm your whereabouts? Do you have an alibi, sir?'

The Mayor swallowed hard. His eyes darted all around the room, not knowing which way to look.

Just then, two policemen burst through the door, swinging it wide open. I recognised them. They were from neighbouring Cascade Point.

'Mayor Kevin Ludwick, you're under arrest for theft,' the big one said, as they strode towards him. 'We have an eyewitness that places you at the Goodwear jewellery store in Cascade Point last night around midnight, looting the place.'

'Officers,' I yelled, as the little one grabbed Mayor Ludwick. 'Scoop McLaren from *Click!* Are you absolutely certain?'

'We have an eyewitness that places him at the scene. And we have CCTV footage that places him at three other robberies over the past two months. He's been in cahoots with the Mayor of Cascade Point.'

Ah! The voice on the other end of the car park conversation!

'The pair have been enjoying quite a lucrative little crime spree,' the policeman continued. 'All of this is off the record, of course. We'll release a statement to the media shortly.'

I nodded. 'Thank you, officer.'

They led him to the door and began pushing through the throng of stunned townspeople.

'What's going on?' the milkman asked. 'Is he Sonny Fink or not?'

'You fools,' Mayor Ludwick spat, as the police led him away. 'I'm not Sonny Fink. Not at all! I was too busy robbing jewellery stores! You were all on my back about leading the charge to uncover Sonny Fink, while I was preoccupied planning my next robbery! Sonny Fink was the last thing on my mind!'

'But why, Kev?' Dad asked, bewildered, following on his heels.

Ludwick huffed. 'Do you know how much money mayors make, Ted?' he asked.

'Obviously not enough,' Dad replied, shaking his head.

Mayor Ludwick was almost out on the street when he turned back to the crowd.

'I may be a thief,' he shouted to anyone who would listen, 'but an evil newspaper editor, I am not!'

By this time the office was abuzz. Mrs Lumgarten fainted with all the excitement and Dad and I were left to calm the crowd.

'Listen up, everyone,' Dad called.

The crowd slowly quietened.

'What do we do now, Ted? Scoop?' Mrs Bailey called. 'If Ludwick's not Fink then… who is?'

By this time the room was silent. Everywhere I looked, eyes were upon me, searching for answers. Answers that I didn't have. I'd never felt so out of my depth.

I grabbed Dad's hand and he squeezed it.

'Well—' Dad started out.

'Wait, Dad,' I told him. 'I'll do it.'

I let go of Dad's hand and stepped forward. Higgity Harbour was counting on me. They trusted me. I'd never let them down before and I wasn't about to start now.

'I'll tell you what we do now,' I said in the loudest voice I could conjure. 'We stick together, as a community. We keep our ears pricked and our eyes peeled.'

I looked behind to Dad. He smiled and gave me an encouraging nod to keep going.

'Sonny Fink lives among us, this we know. And

it'll only be a matter of time before this rogue editor slips up. So if anyone sees or hears anything out of the ordinary, anything at all, please contact either myself, my reporter Evie Andrews, Deputy Mayor Tom Willis or my dad, Ted McLaren.'

As I looked out into the crowd, and at all the eyes looking back at me, I faked a smile.

I wanted them to have confidence in me, and I knew in my heart that I *would* do whatever it took to save my community. But I also knew that Mayor Ludwick, just like my dad, was *not* Sonny Fink.

We had run out of suspects.

CHAPTER SEVEN

AN OPEN LETTER TO SONNY FINK

By Scoop Mclaren

To the editor of *The Dark Times*, Sonny Fink, I say this…

We will find you and then the awful hold that you have over this town with your terrible newspaper will end.

We will not stop until you are caught. We will leave no stone unturned.

The citizens of Higgity Harbour are no longer willing to stand by and let you wreak havoc on our little coastal paradise.

We are coming for you.

You have been warned.

Readers are reminded that while *Click!* does not deliver the news before it happens, we maintain the highest of journalistic standards and can be trusted to report the truth, always!

After appealing to the community for any information that might lead to Sonny Fink's identity, leads came flowing in from all over the place, but unfortunately nothing panned out.

Evie and I took to the streets of Higgity Harbour with our voice recorders, interviewing residents and scouring for clues. Anything that might lead us to uncovering the identity of *The Dark Times* editor.

I stopped Mrs Bailey as she was leaving Frank Franklin's butcher shop.

'Mrs Bailey, Scoop McLaren, *Click!*' I said.

Mrs Bailey rolled her eyes.

'I know very well who you are, young lady,' she said, sitting her bag of pork sausages down on the cobblestone pavement. 'I used to change your nappies when you were a baby!'

I felt my face go pink as Evie giggled.

Pressing the record button on my voice recorder, I held it up to Mrs Bailey's mouth. She frowned as she stared down at it.

'What's this all about, then, hey? Am… am I being interrogated?' she asked.

'Not at all. I simply want to know if you've seen or heard anything suspicious of late,' I told her.

Mrs Bailey went on to blame Iris Lumgarten for being Sonny Fink because her lights came on just before midnight and then went out not long after.

'*Every* single night,' Mrs Bailey said. 'If she's not uploading that horrible newspaper, then what on earth is she doing up at that time?'

Across the street, Evie spied Mrs Lumgarten leaving Betty Wiseman's hair salon, so rushed over to her with the questions.

'Mrs Lumgarten, Evie Andrews, reporter at *Click!*' she said. Then she went on to tell her all about Mrs Bailey's theory.

Mrs Lumgarten was outraged.

She said Doctor Blaxland had put her on a new tablet that made her get up and go to the toilet through the night.

'But I don't want *that* in the paper!' she cried.

Then she blamed Mrs Bailey for being Sonny Fink.

'Why is *she* up at midnight every night looking to see if *I'm* up at midnight every night?' she asked. 'Seems a bit sus to me!'

At the skate park we came across a bunch of year 8 students who were all convinced that school principal,

Mrs Cheryl Bloomflower, was Sonny Fink.

'What makes you say that?' I shouted to Will Bradley as he performed a wicked 360 varial kickflip right before my very eyes.

'Well,' he said, coming down to earth with a steely clunk, 'she's ruining our lives during the school term. Why not ruin our summer holidays too?'

Just to be on the safe side, Evie and I spent two hours that afternoon staking out Mrs Bloomflower's house. It wasn't until her neighbour, Maurice Klaus, asked us what we were doing, that we realised she wasn't even home.

'She's spending the summer in India,' he told us. 'Teaching orphan children how to speak English.'

'Oh... that's... awfully nice,' Evie replied as she crossed CHERYL BLOOMFLOWER off her dwindling list of suspects.

'But I'll tell you who you two *should* be keeping an eye on,' Mr Klaus said.

'Who?' I asked.

'Sid Corman.'

'Sid Corman? But... he's your golf mate? And you two organise the community choir Christmas concert together, every year.'

'Not any more,' he replied, looking around

sheepishly. 'I no longer trust *anyone* around this harbour. No one I tell you.'

And with that, he quietly closed the door in our faces.

Everybody was suspicious of everybody else. Friends who had been friends for years had started doubting each other.

The community needed to stick together at a time like this because divided, we were just easier for Sonny Fink to conquer.

When we told my dad about our full afternoon of interviewing residents, looking for suspects and hunting for clues, he decided to give me extra pocket money so Evie and I could get milkshakes and hot chips at Mr Mack's café. I think he also felt sorry for us because we turned up with zero leads and zero suspects.

Mr Mack was waxing a surfboard when we arrived.

'Well, well, well, if it isn't my two worst customers,' he said, leaning the surfboard against the counter and wiping his hands on a towel. 'What'll it be today? Half a milkshake… between two?'

'It's your lucky day, Mr Mack,' I told him. 'We'll have a chocolate malt milkshake and a plate of chips *each*.'

'*Each?* Wow,' he rolled his eyes. 'Now I'll be able to

buy that mansion in the Caribbean!'

He sulked off into the kitchen as Evie and I found a booth near the door. It was the best spot for the afternoon breeze to blow in and tickle our sun-kissed faces after a hot day of sleuthing.

'Remind me again why we come here,' Evie said. 'Mr Mack's a real fuddy-duddy.'

'We come here for the sea views and the cheapest milkshakes and chips in Higgity Harbour. Forget him. Mr Mack and his bad service is the least of our worries.'

Evie sighed. 'I know. We're all out of suspects, the town's gone mad and Sonny Fink is probably sitting back laughing at us.'

I leaned forward. I'd never seen my feisty little reporter so disheartened. 'Don't give up on me now, Evie. One thing my mum always says is that if you give up, you'll never know if a breakthrough was *just* around the corner.'

'I guess,' she said, leaning back and stretching her tired legs out.

'FEET OFF THE BOOTHS!' Mr Mack yelled from the kitchen.

Evie promptly took her legs down. 'Sheesh,' she said, before quietly adding. 'Fuddy-duddy.'

'And I heard that!' he yelled.

We put our heads down and giggled.

Then Doctor Blaxland walked in.

'Hello, Scoop, Evie. How's our favourite little detective editor and her little roving reporter doing? Caught Sonny Fink yet?' he asked.

As nice as Doctor Blaxland was, from the tone of his voice, I could tell that he did *not* take me or my *little roving reporter* seriously as investigative journalists.

'We're currently working on some leads,' I told him.

'We *are*?' Evie said.

I kicked her shin under the booth.

'Ow!'

'Yes,' I looked at Doctor Blaxland and smiled. 'We are. Currently working on some leads that is.'

He chuckled. 'Good,' he said. 'I'm just here to pick up dinner,' he told us. 'Imogen is simply demanding Mr Mack's hot dogs for dinner. Her mother would have a pink fit. Not the most nutritious meal in the world but, you know my little sapphire, Imogen. Whatever she wants…'

'She gets,' the three of us said in unison.

He laughed again. 'Yes.'

Mr Mack walked out of the kitchen, did a full circle to get the plastic strips that hung in the doorway off himself and brought our milkshakes and chips to the table.

'Yum,' Evie said taking a hot chip from the plate and blowing on it. 'Thanks, Mr Mack. I'm starving.'

'Yeah, yeah,' he said. 'That'll be nine pounds, fifty.'

I took a ten pound note from my pocket and handed it to him. 'Keep the change,' I smiled.

He stared back at me blankly. 'Gee. Thanks,' he said before turning to Doctor Blaxland and nodding. 'Doc.'

'I'll have two of your finest hot dogs, good man, complete with all the trimmings,' Doctor Blaxland said.

'Coming up,' Mr Mack replied, passing back through the plastic strips.

'You know, Scoop,' Doctor Blaxland said, squeezing into the booth next to me, 'you're making quite the impression on my Imogen.'

'I am?' I asked in between sips of my milkshake. 'What do you mean?'

'Your newspaper of course. Imogen's so impressed with your work. So impressed in fact that she's trying her hand at her *own* newspaper.'

Evie looked over the table at me.

'Really?' she said. 'Tell us more.'

'Well, I'm sure she won't mind me telling you that you have inspired her to become an editor herself,

Scoop. Of course, she won't let *me* see it, not yet anyway. Says she's not uploading it until it's absolutely perfect,' he smiled with pride. 'But that's my little sapphire – forever the perfectionist. She's up until past midnight, *every night*, in her bedroom, just working away at—'

Evie spat her milkshake out all over the table at the mention of the word 'midnight'.

I grabbed some napkins and began wiping up. I glared over at Evie who mouthed the word 'sorry' at me.

'*Every* night?' I asked, turning my attention back to Doctor Blaxland. 'At midnight you say?'

'Why, yes, that's right.' He stared at Evie. 'Goodness, dear, are you all right? You've turned a peculiar shade of grey.'

'What? Oh, yes, I'm… fine.'

'And you say that she's never showed you this newspaper?' I asked Doctor Blaxland.

'Yes, that's correct. She said she'd show me when the time was right. God bless her little cotton socks,' he beamed.

'Hey, doc,' Mr Mack called from the counter. 'Your hot dogs are ready.'

Doctor Blaxland shuffled out of the booth. 'Well,

I'll see you girls another time. Remember, Imogen's friends are always welcome in the Blaxland house,' he smiled as he went off to collect his dinner.

'Imogen's *friends*? Working on her newspaper *every night* until after *midnight*!' Evie shook her head. 'Poor Doctor Blaxland. He has no idea… about anything! His daughter could quite possibly be Sonny Fink. Right under his very nose!'

'Imogen Blaxland…. as Sonny Fink?'

'I know, but let's face it, Scoop. We went through just about the entire town today and came up with nothing.'

'You're right. This is the best lead that we have and we must follow it up.'

On the walk home from the surf shack, we devised a plan.

We needed to be outside Imogen's bedroom window at precisely one minute past midnight. If she really was Sonny Fink, we would be there to prove it!

When we let our parents in on our plan of action, there was no way either my dad or Evie's mum would let us out of the house at that hour alone, so we agreed to let Evie's big brother Corey accompany us.

Corey is eighteen, six feet tall and captain of the local rugby team. Nobody in their right mind would dare mess with us while Corey was around.

Evie refers to him as her 'bodyguard', and the pair have always been close. Sometimes it makes me wish that I had a brother or a sister, but I don't think about it all that much.

Although it wasn't forecast, a storm was brewing overhead and by the time Evie and Corey met me on the corner of my street at 11.40 p.m., a lightning show was illuminating the sky.

To make matters worse, the Blaxland's live next to the old cemetery, a place I strive really hard to stay away from ever since I heard the legend of Deadeye Dan. Let alone in the middle of the night. Let alone in the middle of a storm.

'You guys are ten minutes late,' I told them sharply as we headed off. 'Step swiftly. We've got time to make up now.'

I had my mobile phone, my notebook and sparkly silver pen as well as my camera, swinging around my neck. I could see the headline already: *SONNY FINK, CAUGHT IN THE ACT!*

'Blame Evie,' Corey said as the pair tagged alongside me. 'Who does their hair to go out in the dark in the middle of a storm?'

'Well, I do,' Evie smiled under the light of the

very last lamp post.

We were now on the outskirts of town heading into the darkness with only Corey's torch to light the way.

The wind started to pick up and unfortunately for us, it was blowing against our direction making every step a labour.

While the thunder only crackled from a distance, the lightning seemed to be right upon us. With every flash I flinched and I bet Evie did too, but, to our credit, we soldiered on. If we wanted to catch Sonny in the act, or wipe Imogen off our suspect list, we had little choice.

'Do *you* think Imogen Blaxland could be Sonny Fink, Corey?' Evie asked her brother as we trudged along.

She took his hand and I took hers – a strong chain against the wind.

'Sure,' Corey replied. 'Girls can be just as evil as boys. Everybody knows that.'

'I guess,' Evie said.

'Do you two think if your friend really is Sonny Fink and you catch her in the act, it'll wake our dad up?' Corey asked, raising his voice above the howling winds.

'Firstly, she's not our friend, and secondly… I really

hope so,' Evie replied. 'I really miss Dad.'

'Me too. How are we going for time, Scoop?' Corey asked.

I touched my phone: *11.45 p.m.* 'We've got sixteen minutes,' I shouted. 'We better get a hurry on.'

By the time we reached the old cemetery we could see the Blaxland's two-storey house next door, in darkness bar for a dull light illuminating a room downstairs.

'*That's* Imogen's bedroom,' Evie said. 'I remember playing there when I was a little girl.'

'You're *still* a little girl,' Corey chimed and Evie pushed him.

The wind was blowing an absolute gale by now which had really slowed our progress. I looked at my phone. 'Oh no, it's almost midnight!' I cried.

We started to run. Just then a loud crack of thunder rang out, shaking the ground and Evie and I screamed. A heavy downpour of rain followed, hitting our faces like sharp pins.

'We'll have to take a short cut, through the cemetery,' Corey shouted. 'We won't make it in time if we don't!'

Evie and I followed Corey through the rickety old cemetery gates. It was hard work dodging gravestones with only the bouncing light from Corey's torch and the lightning to guide us.

I checked my phone as I ran. 'It's 11.59!' I shouted.

'Run faster!' Evie squealed.

I took off but felt my left foot go down a hole and fall from underneath me. Then my whole body followed. I was on the ground, flat on my face and when I looked up I saw it: HERE LIES DEADEYE DAN, A MORE EVIL PIRATE THERE NEVER TWAS.

Deadeye Dan Durnam's grave!

'Arghhhh,' I shouted.

Evie and Corey stopped. 'Oh no!' Evie cried before turning her head away. 'Don't look at it, Scoop! It's midnight! YOU'LL TURN TO DUST!'

'Get up, Scoop!' Corey bellowed. 'RUN!'

I closed my eyes and raced towards my friends. The three of us scurried through the back gate of the cemetery, finally into the Blaxland's yard.

'Corey,' I shouted. 'You're the fastest!' I took my camera from around my neck and tossed it to him. 'Go! Get a picture. We'll follow!'

Corey caught the camera in his safe rugby hands and raced off ahead.

The wind was so forceful, I could feel it lifting

my jacket. Clumps of wet hair stuck to my face, into my eyes. I brushed it away as Evie held her hand out for me to grab. I took hold of it and together we ran towards Corey, by now just a shadowy figure in the distance.

With each clap of thunder, I squeezed Evie's hand.

'We're almost there, Scoop!' Evie shouted. 'Keep going!'

By the time we reached Imogen's bedroom window, it was two minutes past midnight.

The wind suddenly settled and the rain had also eased considerably.

'Did you get a picture?' I asked Corey as we found him peering through the bedroom window.

'I can't see,' he said. 'It's… it's too dark. There's no sign of movement.'

'Is she in there? Is she Sonny Fink?' Evie asked.

'IS SHE SONNY FINK?' a voice boomed from behind us.

'Arghhhhh!' we all screamed.

As lightning lit up the sky we turned to see Doctor Blaxland standing there wearing a raincoat and a not too pleased look on his face.

'What on earth is going on here?' he cried.

CHAPTER EIGHT

He gave us towels and steamy hot chocolates. My dad would never do this if he caught some kids skulking around outside my bedroom window at midnight!

'I think I'm the most disappointed in you, Corey Andrews,' Doctor Blaxland said, sitting down at the kitchen table across from us. 'Eighteen years old, the captain of the rugby team no less, getting involved in such nonsense.'

'Don't blame me, doc,' Corey said, gulping down his chocolatey drink. 'It was all Scoop and Evie's idea. I'm just the chaperone. Mum made me.'

Then Doctor Blaxland turned his attention to Evie and I. 'And you two. Out, running around in the middle of the night? Out *here*? Why, Scoop? Does your father know about this?'

'Well, Doctor Blaxland,' I started out. I glanced over at Evie and she nodded, encouraging me to continue. 'I'm not quite sure how to break this to you, but we have reason to believe that your daughter... well... she may be Sonny Fink.'

'Sonny Fink? That... horrible newspaper editor? That's simply preposterous,' he said. 'Outrageous... *impossible.* My Imogen cannot be Sonny Fink. She just can't.'

'Why is she up at midnight, every night? And she's Sonny Fink's biggest fan. She told me herself,' I said.

'That's easy,' he replied. 'She's up at midnight every night writing her—' He stopped and then he frowned as the realisation sunk in. 'Writing... her newspaper.'

'Exactly. A newspaper she's never showed you,' I softly told him.

He just sat there, staring blankly at the kitchen table.

'Would I be able to speak with her? Please?' I asked.

Doctor Blaxland stood up. 'I'll go get her and... she can answer your questions,' he said as he despondently moped off.

Evie and I looked at each other tentatively as Corey took one last huge gulp of his hot chocolate. He sat the mug down and wiped his mouth.

'Boy, you two really know how to bring people down,' he said, shaking his head.

'Corey Arthur Andrews,' Evie quipped and was about to give her brother a blast when we heard Doctor Blaxland screaming from Imogen's bedroom.

I'd never heard a grown man cry out like that before. Not in real life anyway. It was dreadful!

I leapt to my feet.

'Help! Somebody help!' Doctor Blaxland cried.

Following the screams, we raced down the long hall and into Imogen's room.

The sight that met us sent chills down my spine.

Evie squealed. She ran into her big brother's arms and buried her face in his chest as Doctor Blaxland sat, sobbing at his daughter's feet.

'What's happened to Imogen?' Corey quietly asked, his eyes wide with horror.

'*The Dark Times*,' I said, running over to Imogen's computer.

HIGGITY HARBOUR TEEN TURNED TO STONE

By Sonny Fink

In a turn of events bound to shock locals, Higgity Harbour girl Imogen Blaxland will be turned to stone at precisely one minute past midnight.

Word around the coastal town has it that Miss Blaxland has been hinting that she could be the macabre editor of *The Dark Times*. Obviously, she is not.

There is only one *Dark Times* and there is only one Sonny Fink. Any imposters or copycats will meet with the same fate, so let this be a lesson to all.

To the editor of *Click!*, Scoop McLaren, I say this…

Any further attempts to catch me will only make things worse, of this you can be sure.

If I were you, I would stop with this ridiculous witch hunt and instead focus my energies on dealing with the daily disasters, which will only continue. Make no mistake about that – Sonny Fink is here to stay.

You have no idea what I am capable of, and I am unstoppable. Your crusade to reveal my identity will only end in disaster.

Back off!

I again remind readers that, unlike the *Higgity Harbour Gazette* and *Click!*, *The Dark Times* is the ONLY newspaper that will deliver the news to you before it happens.

Dad came and picked us up from Doctor Blaxland's house.

Before we left, Doctor Blaxland begged me to find Sonny Fink and bring his daughter back to him. I looked into his sad, desperate eyes and told him that I'd try my very best.

'This has been the worst night ever,' Evie said, sitting next to me in the back seat. 'You almost got turned to dust and poor Imogen *did* get turned to stone.' She leaned back and sighed. 'Poor Imogen.'

We sailed along in silence from that point. Not only did I not want to speak, I didn't have anything to say. I felt helpless.

The storm had all but disappeared, with nothing left but tiny droplets of rain falling sporadically on my window as I stared out into the darkness.

'You ok back there, Henley?' Dad asked.

'Yes, Dad,' I replied.

'Not thinking of giving up now, are you?'

Even though it was dark, I could just feel Evie and Corey staring at me, anxious to hear my answer.

Finally I said: 'No, Dad. Not at all.'

'That's my girl,' he replied and I could tell from the sound of his voice that he was smiling.

Then my phone chimed. I looked down at the screen.

Holey, moley!

'I just got a… a friend request,' I stammered.

'So?' Evie replied. 'I get them all the time. Who's it from? And why is your voice shaking?'

I swallowed down hard.

'It's from… Sonny Fink.'

Dad slammed the brakes on so hard, Corey nearly went through the windscreen.

'Jeez, Mr McLaren!' he cried. 'Steady up!'

'Oh, sorry, son,' Dad said as he pulled off the road.

'Well,' Evie urged me, 'go ahead. Friend Sonny.'

'What? No! I don't want people to see me being *friends* with Sonny Fink.'

She huffed. 'You won't *really* be friends, but you might be able to go through the profile. Find out a bit more.'

With the press of a button, I accepted Sonny Fink's friend request. Then we went to work at scouring the profile.

'Anything there, love? Any clues as to Sonny's identity?' Dad asked.

'No, nothing. No information, no contact details, nothing.'

My phone chimed again.

'Oh, boy,' I said.

'What?' Dad asked.

‘I just got a message. From Sonny Fink.’

‘Well, read it!’ Evie said, bouncing up and down excitedly. ‘What does it say?’

Gulping down hard, I opened the message.

Roses are red,
Violets are blue,
Keep chasing after me, Scoop McLaren,
And just watch what happens to you.

Evie gasped, Dad and Corey held their breaths and I could feel my stomach whirl with a mixture of fear and anger.

♥

The very next morning after Imogen got turned to stone, Evie and I sat in the library discussing our next move.

‘Well, that’s another suspect we can cross off our list,’ Evie said, folding her legs underneath her on the chair. ‘Poor Imogen, poor… horrible Imogen.’

‘I know. I’m not Imogen’s biggest fan but never in a million years would I wish her harm,’ I said.

‘Me neither.’

'But don't worry, Evie. My guess is that when we find Sonny Fink, Imogen will be returned to normal.'

'And my dad too,' she smiled. 'Oh, I really hope so.' She looked around before whispering, 'What about the message from Sonny?' Then she tilted her head to one side. 'Are you scared, Scoop? You can tell me if you are.'

I sighed. 'I guess I am… a little. But I also think it could be a good thing.'

'Why?'

'The only reason Sonny Fink threatened me is because of the fear that we're getting closer. That's why we just have to keep going, Evie. If Sonny's getting nervous, we *must* be getting closer.'

'Right. But where to now? Or *who* to now?'

Just then Miss Jennings appeared and scared the jeepers out of us. She was always creeping around in her size nine, flat shoes that never made a sound.

She placed both hands on the desk we were sitting at and leaned in towards us.

'You know I wouldn't normally bother wasting my breath talking to you two little bacilli,' she started out, 'but in light of that poor, ginger-headed girl being turned to stone, I simply must speak up.'

'All right,' I told her curiously. 'We're listening.'

'I was at the Mayor's office yesterday and I feel I

have some information which may be of help to you in your pursuit of Sonny Fink.'

It wasn't like Miss Jennings to be helpful, but I guess because of the catastrophic situation we all found ourselves in, even horrible, sarcastic librarians would pitch in and help if it meant ridding the town of Sonny Fink.

Evie pulled out her notebook. 'If you know something, shoot,' she said. 'We're all out of leads.'

I could've kicked her under the table. Even if you *are* all out of leads, a good journalist never divulges this to the general public. It erodes trust.

I jumped in. 'Actually, we do have a few avenues we are currently following up,' I told Miss Jennings as Evie frowned in confusion, 'but any information is welcome.'

'I don't want it recorded,' she said, folding her arms. 'I don't want my name mentioned. This is strictly off the record.'

'Oh, of course,' I told her, gesturing for Evie to put her notebook away.

'Ok.' Miss Jennings sighed heavily. 'Here is what I know.'

She pulled out a chair and sat down next to me. I don't think I'd ever been this close to Miss Jennings before. She looked prettier close up and smelled nice – like pineapple mixed with gardenias.

'I think I know who Sonny Fink is,' she said.

'Who?' Evie and I asked in unison.

'It's...'

She looked around.

'There's no one else in the library, Miss Jennings,' Evie said, rolling her eyes. 'Apart from Scoop and me, there is *never* anyone else in the library.'

'All right. Sonny Fink is…'

'*Is?*' I urged.

'Kenny Dixon,' she said.

I nearly fell off my chair.

'Kenny Dixon?' Evie said, laughing. 'Knuckle-head Kenny Dixon? Eats worms for a pound each on a dare? Sports mad? Rarely thinks, or talks, about anything else? Rides on the wrong side of the footpath? Fell off the stage at last year's awards presentation? Kenny Dixon? *That's* your evil mastermind?'

Evie had a point. A good one. Kenny was nice and all, the son my dad never had (and never really wanted), but I would be very surprised if he had it in him to write his own name and address on the back of an envelope, let alone the front page of a newspaper every night.

'You're loopy,' Evie told Miss Jennings, before slumping back in her seat with disappointment. 'I thought you really had something. You're just being silly.'

'Silly, am I?' Miss Jennings whipped around and got right up in Evie's face. To Evie's credit, she didn't even flinch. 'I've simply put two and two together and—'

'Come up with five?' Evie said. 'If Kenny Dixon is Sonny Fink, then I'm The Cat in the Hat.'

I could see the anger building as Miss Jennings' eye started to twitch. She was about to tear strips off Evie.

I tried to calm the situation.

'We can't discount anyone, Evie,' I said. 'Go on, Miss Jennings. What makes you think Kenny Dixon is Sonny Fink?'

'Well, apart from it being completely not obvious, and I read a lot of crime novels – it's always the completely *not obvious* ones...'

'Go on.'

'He's been borrowing books on journalism.'

'That doesn't sound like something Kenny would do,' I said.

'No. And watch this.'

Miss Jennings pulled out her smartphone.

'I've got the library surveillance system on an app on my phone. Every night, at around 11.30 p.m., Kenny climbs through the back window with the broken lock and uses the computer.'

Evie and I watched as Kenny sneaked through the window, set himself up at the library's main computer, and began typing.

'Wow,' Evie said. 'Look at the time stamp – 11.30 p.m.'

'Told you,' Miss Jennings said.

She forwarded thirty-two minutes and we watched as Kenny left the computer.

'He gets up and leaves at precisely two minutes past midnight, giving him enough time to come in, write his despicable headlines, post the newspaper to the web at one minute past midnight, and then he leaves.'

'And he does this every night?' I asked.

Miss Jennings nodded. 'Yes. Every single night for the past two months.' She waved her phone in front of my face. 'And I've got the cold, hard evidence to prove it.'

Evie and I looked at each other. This had the makings of a good lead.

'As much as I think Kenny's kind of, sort of, an ok human being, this doesn't look good,' Evie said.

'What do you think, Scoop?'

I needed to gather my thoughts. On the one hand, I was grateful to have another suspect, seemingly the best one to date, but on the other hand I was so totally disappointed in Kenny. How could he do this to me and my dad? Especially my dad. What reason could he possibly have for wanting to destroy us and our town?

As if to read my mind, Miss Jennings turned to me.

'I know what you're thinking,' she said, 'but sometimes people just aren't who they seem. Sometimes they put on a clever act to hide who they really, truly are.'

Then she rested her (surprisingly) warm hand on mine as a half-smile crossed her face.

I had never liked Miss Jennings – I don't think anyone in the history of Higgity Harbour ever had – but at that moment, I did appreciate the gesture.

'Dixon needs to be caught,' she said, squeezing my hand tighter, 'like a mouse in a trap. *Snap!*'

Evie and I both jumped.

'If you can get him in the same room as you at exactly one minute past midnight tonight, with no computer and no way to release that disastrous newspaper of his, you'll have found your Sonny Fink.'

CHAPTER NINE

By the time I got home, Dad had already taken off to his golf club meeting and I didn't get the chance to tell him about Kenny.

He left a note saying that it would probably be a late one. Tom Willis was turning sixty and they would have a drink to celebrate after the meeting.

Evie was allowed to sleep over at my house and it was about ten o'clock in the evening when Kenny knocked on the front door. I had invited him over, telling him that we had important newspaper business to discuss.

'Leave all the talking to me, Scoop,' Evie said, as I went for the door. 'You're too close to this one. Kenny's like... your brother.'

'Ewwww,' I replied. 'He is not! He's like my... dad's paper boy.'

Kenny wasn't in a good mood. I could tell that

from the get-go. I ushered him in, locked the front door and told him to take a seat in the lounge. He trudged all the way down the hall.

'Why'd you call me over here at this time of night?' he asked, plonking down on the sofa. 'And what's Evie doing here?'

'Got somewhere *better* to be, do you?' Evie asked.

'What? What'd you say that for?'

'Because, Kenny Dixon,' Evie said, circling the sofa, 'if that's even your real name, we think—'

'Hold on a second, Evie,' I jumped in. '*I'll* handle this.'

'Handle what?' Kenny rolled his eyes. He got up and started pacing. A sure sign of nerves, my dad always said. 'You two are acting weird, and if somebody doesn't start giving me some answers as to exactly why I'm here in a year 7's house at ten o'clock on a Wednesday night, I'm going. I've got better things to do.'

'Oh, we *allll* know about your *better things*, Kenny Dixon. *If* that's even your real name,' Evie said.

'That's it,' Kenny said, turning on his heel, 'I'm outta here.'

I stepped in front of him. 'You... you can't go,' I told him. 'You need to stay. Until midnight.'

'Midnight?!' he roared. 'Why? I... I can't.' He looked at his watch. 'I've got some other place I need to be.'

He tried to make a beeline for the door.

'The library?' I asked.

He spun back around, swallowed hard and stared right at me.

'How... how do you know about that?' he stammered hoarsely. 'Nobody... nobody's supposed to know about that.'

'Sit down, Kenny,' I told him.

Kenny swore black and blue that he wasn't Sonny Fink, but of course he would, wouldn't he?

'What *are* you on about, Scoop? Does your dad know you've kidnapped me?' he asked.

'We know all about your nightly trips to the library, Kenny. Miss Jennings told us that—'

'Miss Jennings? You're actually listening to that old bat?'

'The evidence is stacked against you, Kenny,' Evie piped up. 'If you're not Sonny Fink, then why do you break into the library each night at eleven-thirty and then leave at two minutes past midnight, hey? You've got to admit, it looks a bit suspicious.'

'I don't *break in*, the window is always unlocked. And it's none of your beeswax why I go there every night.'

He turned to me. 'When's your dad getting home? You are going to be in so much trouble over this.'

'Forget about my dad, Kenny, he can't help you,' I said. 'The only thing that's going to help you now is time.'

'Time? What do you mean *time*?'

'You're going to stay right here until one minute past midnight. If you really *aren't* Sonny Fink, then the paper will come out as normal. But if you are, you can hardly release the next issue while you're sitting here with Evie and me.'

'You've lost it,' he said. 'You've really lost the plot now, Scoop. I used to think you were all right. When my mates told me not to talk to the nerd from the newspaper, I stuck up for you. I even invited you to basketball. Well, now I see that my friends were right about you – you are a boring little nerd who's about to chase up the last of her stupid stories.'

He went over and sat in my dad's favourite chair, checked his watch and then folded his arms.

I didn't show it, I *couldn't* show it because I had to be professional, but Kenny's words hurt.

I know I'm not an ordinary kid. I know I probably take the news too seriously at times, but it's what I do and it's something that I do well.

Evie came over and put her arm around me.

'Are you ok?' she asked quietly. 'Boys are mean. Especially older boys. And *especially* older boys who are probably Sonny Fink.' She glared at Kenny, who poked his tongue out in retaliation.

As much as I appreciated Evie's kindness, I shrugged her off.

I walked over to Kenny, got in his face and said, '*Why* do you go to the library and stay past midnight?'

'I told you – it's none of your business,' he replied. 'But I'll stay. I'll stay and show you two exactly how wrong you both are about me. Stupid girls.'

♥

I reckon it took about two months for the clock to get to midnight.

Not one of us spoke until Kenny finally said, 'You know, while you two twits have got me holed up here, the *real* Sonny Fink is out there somewhere, on the loose.'

'We'll see,' I replied.

Evie tugged on my sleeve. 'Ah, Scoop?'

Kenny and I both turned to her.

'What?'

She was as white as a sheet. She turned her back on Kenny and whispered, 'I think we need to call your dad.'

'Why?'

'Because it's two minutes past midnight and... '

She pointed to the inbox on my laptop.

For the first time since this whole sorry saga began, *The Dark Times* did *not* get delivered.

♥

I didn't upload a paper today.

It feels really strange not to write one but it also feels right. Sonny Fink is caught and I just need to take a well-earned break. I'm sure my loyal readers will understand.

Besides, I really need time to process the fact that Kenny Dixon is Sonny Fink, the dark editor who has been making life in Higgity Harbour miserable for months. I still can't believe it.

Kenny – the boy who stopped to help me fix the flat tyre on my bike even though it would mean being late for football practice. The one who always stuck up for me when the other kids would chant, 'Scoop, Scoop, smells like soup!' He was my friend, but all the while plotting to destroy us. I just don't understand. Why would Kenny do such a thing?

I slept in until nine o'clock, and then I spent a few hours walking Mrs Lumgarten's dog. Dad won't let me have a dog of my own. He says I'm too busy with the paper to look after a dog properly. He's probably right.

Kenny said the books on journalism and the late-night computer sessions were all about him wanting to write a sports column for my dad's paper. He said he was too embarrassed to tell anybody because we've always thought of him as being a bit of a meathead. He said he wouldn't approach my dad until he knew how to be a *real* sports journalist. That was his story and he was sticking to it. I'd never heard such nonsense!

I think the dumb act was to cover up for the fact that he really is an evil journalistic genius, and right under our noses, too.

In any case, I have to wait for the police to interrogate him so I can get the full facts of the matter before I can even think about writing a story to tell the world that Kenny Dixon is Sonny Fink.

I think Dad kind of half-believes Kenny, though. At least I think Dad *wants* to believe him. He always did have a soft spot for Kenny.

♥

Dad was putting the finishing touches on next Monday's issue of the *Gazette* when I got home from my walk.

I'm pleased to say that Dad started caring about stories again, and not just boring old council stories.

'What's front page?' I asked, as I spun around on the old chair in his office. I've been doing that since I was about three.

'A feature on shonky tradesmen,' he said. 'Rick Proctor got ripped off by a dodgy plumber. Now every toilet in his house leaks. We're going to Consumer Affairs about this one.'

I smiled as I watched Dad go through the article with a fine-toothed comb. He looked over at me.

'What are you smiling about?' he asked.

'It's good to have you back, Dad. I wouldn't like to be in that shonky plumber's shoes!'

'Me neither, love,' he replied. 'Where's your roving reporter, on the ground? I thought you two would be busy working on tomorrow's issue.'

I sighed. 'Evie's bummed out big time. She thought that once we caught Sonny Fink her dad would wake up, since it was the raining frogs Sonny wrote about that caused it.'

'Still asleep, hey?'

'Yep. And I ran into Doctor Blaxland this morning while I was out walking Mrs Lumgarten's dog. He was frightfully upset because Imogen's still set in stone too. Weird, isn't it?'

Dad left the paper and spun around in his chair to face me.

'Well, it wouldn't be weird if…'

'If what?'

'If Sonny Fink were still at large. What if Kenny really is innocent like he says, and the real Sonny Fink is just laying low until this all blows over?'

'But the paper didn't come out, Dad! Kenny was with us and the paper didn't come out. He's been secretly studying and writing and sneaking into the library to use the computer… at the exact same time *The Dark Times* comes out. All the evidence points to Kenny, and you always taught me that evidence doesn't lie.'

Dad got up and began to pace. I'd seen my father work before. He'd written plenty of explosive, front-page stories over the years that usually started out with him pacing in his office.

'I know what the evidence says, and I know what

I've always taught you, but—'

Then he tripped. One second he was up, the next he was down, falling face-first on the carpet with a stack of newspapers collapsing on top of him.

'Owwww. Oh… bum!' he yelled.

I rushed to help.

'Are you ok?'

Dad nodded, with a sigh.

'You know, Dad, you wouldn't have this problem if you went digital. You wouldn't have mountains of newspapers falling all over you if you just went digital!'

He looked down. He'd tripped on Kenny's paper-delivery bag.

'I told that boy a thousand times to hang this bag up when he's finished with it. Which reminds me – looks like you'll have to do the paper run from now on.'

'Great,' I huffed.

'Hang on,' Dad said, reaching into the bag. 'What's this?' He pulled out a crumpled piece of paper. 'It's… an article,' he said. 'An article about rugby. Written by… Kenny Dixon.'

I jumped up. 'No way, let me see!'

RUGBY STAR GETS HIS CHANCE ON NATIONAL STAGE

By Kenny Dixon

Higgity Harbour High School's lightning-fast rugby star Marty Collins will join with the cream of the country's junior rugby talent at Big Top Park in Snubsville next week. Collins will line up for the Dangrove Demons and take on the likes of Knockout Bay, Hurtsville and Runaway Cove for the right to hold aloft the Invincible Shield trophy.

The trip to Snubsville marks the end of a huge season for Collins, with the year 10 student having begun his campaign last summer when he took part in pre-season training with the Big-eyed Bulls.

'He didn't finish,' I said.

'I don't think he needs to,' Dad replied. 'This is fantastic. I… I'd give this kid a run as my sports journo any day. I can't believe it!'

A shiver ran down my spine as I processed exactly what this half-written article really meant.

'He was telling the truth all along,' I told Dad. 'He really *does* want to be a sports journalist. That's why he borrowed the books and that's why he sneaked into the library at night when no one would see him. His mum won't let him have a computer at home and the school's closed for the holidays.'

Dad slumped down on his chair and stared at the crumpled piece of paper.

'We weren't dealing with a rogue editor at all,' he said. 'We were dealing with a very talented young man who just didn't believe in himself. Oh, no!'

I went over and rested my hand on Dad's shoulder.

'Don't feel bad, Dad. You had doubts about Kenny being Fink all along, I know you did. I, on the other hand, was so busy trying to prove myself to everyone that I… I messed up. Totally.'

'Don't you be too hard on yourself either, Henley. The evidence *did* point to Kenny. But I guess sometimes evidence *can* be wrong.'

'Sonny Fink is still out there, right, Dad?'

I felt a hot tear fall from my eye and stream down my face.

Dad put his arms around me and gave me a squeeze.

'Afraid so, love.'

CHAPTER TEN

To avoid a mass hysteria in Higgity Harbour, Dad and I kept the fact that Sonny Fink was still roaming around, among us, a secret.

Evie met us at Kenny Dixon's house about fifteen minutes later.

Kenny's mum answered the door.

'Mrs Dixon, we have reason to believe that your son is not in fact Sonny Fink,' Dad told her, after she ushered us inside.

I could see the relief on her face. 'Oh, Ted, I knew it, I knew it all along,' she said. 'Not my Kenny. My Kenny is such a good boy.'

'And a great writer,' Dad said, as he pulled out the dog-eared article. 'Mrs Dixon, your son has been sneaking into the library at night to write stories, that is for certain.'

'To write stories?' She frowned.

'Yes. But he's *not* Sonny Fink. He's actually a pretty decent sports writer. I would go so far as to say that he has a real future in journalism.'

Dad offered her the article and she read it through.

She frowned again. 'My Kenny? My Kenny wrote this? The boy who ate glue until he was eleven?' she asked.

'Yes. I found it in his paper-delivery bag in my office. I can't believe he didn't give it to me. It's good, isn't it?'

'My Kenny, a sports journalist!' Kenny's mum beamed.

'Yes, indeed. Can you let Kenny know that we are here to see him?'

Kenny was actually surprisingly forgiving. A lot more forgiving than I think I'd have been if I were accused of being an evil literary mastermind.

'I knew you'd all eventually come to your senses,' he told us, as we sat on his front doorstep. 'So I just hung around in my room reading football magazines, waiting for that to happen. I'm just relieved the *real* Sonny Fink has gone underground. And maybe that's where Fink will stay from now on—? What do you think, Mr M?'

Dad shook his head. 'In all my years of reporting

on crime, I'm yet to come across a criminal who just… stops.'

'Well, I'm *very* relieved Kenny's not Fink,' Evie said.

Kenny huffed. 'You and me both.'

'I mean, if we catch the *real Sonny* then there's a good chance my dad will wake up for real, I just know it. Don't you think, Mr McLaren?'

'There's a good possibility, Evie,' Dad said.

'But where do we start?' she cried. 'We're all out of suspects, we're all out of leads.'

'Whatever we do, we have to do it fast,' I said. 'It's only a matter of time before Fink finds out that Kenny is innocent and that we're back out on the hunt.'

'Mum's already told Iris Lumgarten,' Kenny said. 'And Mrs Bailey.'

'Then we don't have much time at all.'

Then my phone chimed.

'A message,' Evie said, jumping to her feet. 'From Fink?'

I looked down at the screen and felt myself gasp.

'Yes,' I told them.

'Well? What does it say?' Kenny asked.

Scoop McLaren,
No more rhymes.

No more of this nonsense.

This ends tonight.

Meet me at the old abandoned warehouse near the wharf. 11 p.m. Sharp.

And bring your band of nitwits with you.

♥

I won't lie. I'd never been so scared. Not in my whole entire life.

Not even the time when the travelling reptile exhibit came to our school when I was six, and I got volunteered to have them wrap a giant adder around my neck.

Dad says it's ok (and perfectly normal) to be scared sometimes. Even he gets scared and he's a grown man. It's ok to be scared, just don't let the fear stop you, he said.

There's *no way* I'm letting Sonny Fink scare me away.

We arrived at the abandoned warehouse by the wharf at precisely 10:58 p.m. It was once used to store cargo but container ships don't pass this way any more. Now it (barely) stands, an old, dilapidated building, out of the way and forgotten.

'All right, kids,' Dad said as we stood outside. 'Whatever we do, we stick together. Got it?'

We nodded.

'No one strays away.'

'Right, Mr M,' Kenny said.

'Agreed. We stay together,' said Evie, taking hold of my hand.

Then Dad turned to me. 'Henley? No heroics. All right?'

Dad knows me well!

I nodded. 'Right, Dad.'

'What's the plan, Mr M?' Kenny asked.

'Well, the plan. Right. It's... um...'

Oh jeez, I don't think Dad has a plan.

I stepped forward. 'The plan is to find out who Sonny Fink is and what it will take for the disastrous headlines to stop. That's the plan. This is a golden opportunity, one that might not pass our way again. We can't blow it.'

'Right,' Dad agreed as we forged off, single file, towards the warehouse doors. 'And... don't forget to stick together!'

Dad pushed open the old wooden door to the warehouse, the sound of the singing hinges cutting through the otherwise still and silent night. Once the door was open, we all stood back and peered inside.

It was pitch black apart from six large windows that lined the back wall, each one illuminated by the moonlight behind it.

I took out my torch as we slowly made our way inside. The warehouse was cold, the air had a dampness to it, and it smelled like off fish.

I quickly found that the torch wasn't much help. The warehouse was too big for the light to illuminate any more than a few metres in front of us, still it was better than the eerie complete darkness.

The warehouse had been abandoned for as long as my dad could remember. The floorboards creaked as we crept along. I guessed they were probably rotting from the salt air and had been doing so for some time.

As if reading my thoughts, Kenny leaned over to me and whispered, 'I hope we don't fall through.'

'Don't say that!'

Apart from the four of us, there was no other sign of life inside and I began to get a sinking feeling in the pit of my stomach. I suspected we'd been duped!

'Come out, Fink,' I called, as we walked around, my voice echoing in the darkness. 'Honour your word. We are here, just like you asked. Show yourself!'

Nothing. Nothing but the faint hint of a gentle sea

breeze picking up outside.

'Huh, figures,' Kenny said. 'Why were we ever so stupid to think that Fink would actually show?'

But then, *'Eeeeekkkkkk!'* Evie cried.

'What is it, Evie?' I asked.

'Over there!' She pointed to the windows. 'Something just fled past, like a ghost. I saw it!'

'Stay still,' I said as I started to walk towards the windows.

'Henley!' Dad whispered loudly. 'Be careful!'

As I grew nearer to the back wall it wasn't the fact that I could *see* anything, but I could certainly sense it. Another soul, breathing shallow breaths, waiting in the darkness. Someone was definitely there, lurking in the shadows.

'Here I am, Fink,' I said slowly. 'Like you said, this ends tonight. Come and get me.'

I lifted my torch and shone it around. Nothing. Nothing but the light dancing in darkness.

Suddenly I felt myself taken aback as a tall, willowy figure rushed past me, a sugary scent lingering in their wake, throwing my torch on the floor. It was pitch-dark. I reached out to grab the culprit only to have Fink's cold, bony hand touch mine and push me away while fleeing. I fell backwards.

'Henley?' Dad shouted. 'What's happened? Are you all right?'

'Fink's on the move!' I yelled from the floor, but there was no use. Fink was no sooner past me than past the others and out the door. Then we heard a *bang!* The sound of the door being closed. And then locked! I crawled on the floor towards the door when I felt a small plastic thing. I picked it up and shuffled it into my pocket.

I got up and ran over to meet Dad, Kenny and Evie who were all madly banging on the door.

'Oh, no!' Kenny cried, thumping the wall. 'We're locked in!'

'Stand back,' Evie said, as she lined herself up. One, two, three steps and… *ka-boom!* The door was karate-kicked open and we all piled outside.

Nice work, Evie!

'Ah, nowhere to be seen,' Dad said, kicking the ground.

'This was a whole waste of time,' Kenny added. 'Fink wins again.'

'No,' I stammered in between laboured breaths. 'Two things I now know for sure, thanks to Sonny Fink.'

'What, Scoop?' Evie asked. 'What could you

possibly know from what just happened in there? Fink led us into a dark warehouse and tried to lock us away. End of story.'

'No, not the end of the story, Evie. *I'll* be the one ending this story. Sonny Fink made a big mistake inviting us to this warehouse.'

'What do you mean, love?' Dad asked. 'Tell us what you know.'

'I now know exactly *who* Sonny Fink is,' I told them, 'and I also know Sonny's next move.'

CHAPTER ELEVEN

It was really getting late, about 11.30 p.m.

'You're sure, Henley? Absolutely certain?' Dad asked as we made our way through the town on foot.

The streets were empty. Higgity Harbour residents were probably all at home, safely tucked away in their beds, blissfully unaware of the horrible fate that was awaiting them.

'Positive, Dad. I know who Sonny Fink is! Let's walk back towards the town centre and I'm sure this is where we will find *The Dark Times* editor.'

The four of us strode, with purpose, through the streets. I was out front with Dad, Evie and Kenny behind me.

'Sonny Fink is trying to be clever,' I continued. 'Fink knew with Kenny being given the all clear today that it would only be a matter of time before we went searching again. That's why we were summoned to the warehouse. So we could all be locked away, the only four people who stood in the way of Sonny wreaking havoc.'

'So where should we go now?' asked Evie.

I took out the plastic card I had thrown into my pocket earlier. 'Sonny Fink dropped this in the warehouse,' I said, waving it at everyone. 'It's a library pass without a photo. So I think we should head to the library! I know that this is where Sonny Fink is hiding!' I whispered.

We rounded the corner and before us stood the town library. The lights were glowing warmly along the footpath leading up to the entrance outside; it looked so welcoming and inviting. I'd been to the library a million times before, relishing brand new releases from my favourite authors, quietly reading in hidden nooks, but this time was different. This time we were in Sonny Fink territory and we needed to keep our wits about us.

Dad turned to me. 'Henley? Are you thinking what I'm thinking?'

'Yes, Dad,' I replied. 'And we have to move fast.'

We shot up the steps with Kenny and Evie hot on our heels.

'What? What are you guys thinking?' Kenny asked.

'We're thinking that tonight's the night,' I told him. 'That Sonny Fink is getting ready to write a headline to end all headlines.'

The four of us climbed through the library window with the broken lock and landed inside a pitch-black corridor. We crept along, the old floor underfoot sounded like it was groaning, announcing our presence with every step. Apart from that, it was frightfully quiet, even for a library, and the air was thick and stuffy. It felt hard to breathe.

Evie stopped in front of me.

'Evie? What's wrong?' I asked.

'Nothing,' she whispered. 'I… I just need to catch my breath, that's all.'

I grabbed her hand. 'We've got this, ok?' I said.

'Sure thing, Scoop.' We both took a deep breath and pushed on.

We decided to split up into pairs – Dad and me, and Evie and Kenny – to find Sonny.

Evie and Kenny took off to the top floor while Dad and I headed downstairs.

The hall outside the basement was dark and chilly, and the floor continued to creak as we went along. Part of me was secretly hoping that Evie and Kenny would find Sonny first and have dealt with the scoundrel by the time Dad and I got there, but a bigger part of me wanted to find the dark editor myself. I had started this crusade against Sonny Fink, and now I just wanted to finish it!

'I've been thinking, Dad. With all that's been going on, Sonny Fink must have special powers or something,' I said, as we crept along. 'What if Sonny sees us, turns around and *bam!* Puts a spell on us?'

'I think Sonny's pretty powerless outside writing the newspaper, love, but let's be careful just in case.'

From a crack under the basement door, we could see light.

'This is it,' Dad whispered. 'Sonny's in there.'

I gulped hard. 'Are you scared, Dad?' I asked.

'To be honest, love, I'm petrified,' he said.

'Me, too.'

'But never mind that now. This is it. This is what we've been waiting for. Ready?'

'As I'll ever be.'

'Right. On the count of three.'

I put my hand on the door handle. I could feel my heart beating in my ears.

'One...' Dad whispered.

I slowly and quietly turned the handle.

'Two...'

I breathed in deeply. I was so glad Dad was with me.

'Three!'

I swung open the door and we raced in.

'Got ya!' I cried.

But the room was empty. Empty apart from a computer sitting on a table in the corner.

'Dad, look!' I cried, running over to it. 'It's the front page of *The Dark Times,* and it's just been finished!'

Dad looked around while I sat down, at the screen. 'Where is Sonny?' he asked.

'I don't know,' I replied, as I read the headline. 'But we've got a bigger problem.'

HIGGITY HARBOUR DESTROYED BY CYCLONE

By Sonny Fink

The idyllic coastal town of Higgity Harbour will be destroyed by a massive cyclone today.

A ferocious storm screaming in off the Celtic Sea will flatten everything and everyone in its path.

Rescue workers will be powerless to help. With no warning, the cyclone will hit at precisely one minute past midnight while residents sleep, blissfully ignorant, in their beds. Overturned cars will rest wherever the wind tosses them, trees will be uprooted, houses demolished and Main Street businesses reduced to rubble.

The lines of communication will be cut, and for those who don't perish in the storm, help will not be rendered in time.

This will be the darkest day in the town's history – the day Higgity Harbour is wiped off the map.

Readers are reminded that *The Dark Times* is the only newspaper to deliver the news before it happens.

We heard the basement door slam shut behind us.

'It's the exclusive of the decade,' Sonny Fink said, as we turned to see… Miss Jennings standing there.

She had Evie and Kenny. Their hands were tied behind their backs and their feet were bound together.

'I found these two wandering aimlessly around the self-help section,' she said. She pushed them towards us and Dad grabbed them both before they fell.

Kenny turned to me. 'Sorry, Scoop,' he said. 'Sonny Fink's stronger than she looks.'

I looked at my watch – it was fifteen minutes until midnight.

I had to act and act fast.

'The sugary scent in the warehouse – pineapple

mixed with gardenias. The plastic library card. It was you. All along, it was you,' I said.

She smiled in an irritatingly smug way. 'Yes, me. All along!'

'The jig's up, Fink,' I told her. 'This ends tonight.'

'Oh, I agree, *Scoop*,' she said, backing us into a corner. 'This *does* end tonight. At one minute past midnight.'

'What did we ever do to you?' Evie cried. 'Why are you so... *mean*?'

'Silence!' Miss Jennings said. 'This is between me and the girl editor.'

'Me? What do you mean, between you and me?' I asked.

'Leave the kids out of it, Fink,' Dad said.

'She's jealous of you, Scoop,' Evie said. 'Your newspaper is the best!' She turned to my dad. 'No offence, Mr McLaren.'

Dad shrugged. 'None taken.'

Sonny started to circle me, menacingly. Toying with me like a cat playing with one of the mice she had unleashed on us. Then she stopped, right in front of me, and glared into my eyes.

'Do you have anything to say for yourself?' she asked. 'All those afternoons sitting in my library, plotting to bring down Sonny Fink, and now here we are.'

I looked up at her. Her face looked older in the dim light of the basement, weathered and worn.

'When you held my hand and were nice to me, when you said people aren't always the way they seem, that sometimes they hide who they truly are, I thought you were talking about Kenny. But you were talking about yourself. That afternoon in the library you made me think there was some good in you, but… there's not,' I said.

'Clever, clever girl,' she smiled wickedly. 'See, there's a reason you're a smarty pants big editor. Unlike your dim-witted father.'

'Hey!' Dad yelled. 'I heard that! And I'll have you know that I just wrote an exposé on dodgy plumbers!'

'Ohhhh, riveting!' she quipped.

Out of the corner of my eye, I could see Evie and Kenny squirming away in the corner, behind Fink. Evie gave me a wink and I knew Kenny was working on loosening her knots.

I had to hold Fink's attention.

'But why?' I asked her. 'Why do you want to destroy Higgity Harbour? It's your home, too.'

'Higgity Harbour?' she spat. 'I have nothing good

to say about Higgity Harbour. Many years ago before your sap of a father moved to town, *I* had a paper, just like yours. *I* was the "Scoop" of my day. But nobody would read my paper. I worked *so* hard to bring those ungrateful plebs in this town the news, but they shunned me! And my editorial career was shattered! They said I only wrote bad news. They said I made half of it up.'

'And did you?' Dad asked.

'Well... yes. But I had to write something! Even if it wasn't altogether true.'

'*That's* where you went wrong,' I told her. 'A good newspaper editor *must* write the truth and *only* the truth. Readers expect nothing less.'

Kenny was still working on Evie's knots, but the minutes were ticking away and fast.

'And you think people want to read *your* sickly sweet headlines?' Fink asked me, drawing closer. 'Your stupid stories about... flower shows and... kiddies' swimming carnivals? No one wants to read that drivel!'

I looked at the clock on the wall – ten minutes until midnight.

'People want to read *bad* news. That's all they're interested in,' she said. 'Good news doesn't sell papers.'

'People are only interested in the *truth* – good *or*

bad,' I told her, 'and that's what I write.'

Behind her, Kenny had done it! He had freed Evie!

'How do you do it, Fink?' I asked her. 'How do you make the headlines happen?'

Miss Jennings paused, then smiled proudly. 'I have amazing abilities that I've turned into wicked, evil abilities. I get it from my grandmother's side.'

'I remember hearing about your grandmother, when I first moved here,' Dad said. 'About how the local kids used to dare each other to walk past her house, frightened she'd put curses on them. But that was all nonsense.'

'Was it?' she spat. 'Ever since I was a little girl, I could see things before they happened. Some call it a psychic ability, others say it's just my dear old granny's blood in my veins. I realised I had the power to cause some real trouble if I wanted to, and who wouldn't? Pretty soon I was controlling my special gift, and it went from seeing things before they happened to *making* things happen every time I would write things down. Bad things.'

'Like when Evie's backpack fell,' I said, wonderingly.

'Right,' she said. 'I see it in my mind and then it just... happens! I went from seeing the future to controlling the future. Which is much more fun, when I can make the future as terrifying as I like.' She smiled evilly.

Evie edged closer to Fink. *Quietly, quietly,* I silently urged. *If she catches you, you're toast!*

'At first I just wrote a story for fun,' Miss Jennings said. 'That day the fog refused to lift—? I pictured the story in my mind, wrote it, and then the next day… it happened!'

'But there's just one thing I don't understand,' I said. 'Why didn't you turn me to stone instead of Imogen? Why didn't you ever write a headline to get rid of *me*? The one person who could stop you?'

'Well where would the fun be in that?' she smirked. 'I wanted to see how long it would take you to find me. And I have to say, I'm a little disappointed. I thought you would have found me long before now!'

I looked at the clock – *five minutes until midnight!*

'The stupid adults in this town were happy to let me be, to wreak havoc, but not you, Scoop McLaren,' she continued. 'You've ruined me and now I'm going to ruin everyone.'

'That's why you wanted us at the warehouse, isn't it? To get us out of the way so you'd be free to come back here and write your very last deadly headline.'

'Precisely! Oh, you're so clever, aren't you, Miss…

Clever Pants?'

'You know, for a writer, you don't have a very varied vocabulary,' I told her.

'Silence!!'

'Again, Fink,' I demanded. *'Why?'*

'You want to know why I did this?'

'Yes!' I cried.

'This is my revenge against the people of Higgity Harbour who destroyed my original newspaper and against you, Scoop because your silly newspaper steals my readership! But when I terrify this town, everyone reads me and knows who the greatest editor is!' she cried. '*The Dark Times* is the best newspaper ever! Writing the news before it even happens – you can't beat that, Scoop McLaren! No one can. Whatever is written in *The Dark Times* happens, and there's nothing anybody can do to stop it. *I* control what happens in this town. When you control the news, you control everything!'

With Evie being a brown belt in karate, I knew she had the strength to push Miss Jennings, well... Sonny Fink over, and the Girl Scout skills to tie her up in no time! Our only hope now was for Dad, Evie and Kenny to hold Fink down while I rewrote the whole front page. But we were running out of time.

Just then Evie jumped out from the shadows.

'Not if *I've* got anything to do with it!' she yelled at Sonny Fink. 'Hi-ya!'

With one perfectly timed side snap kick she knocked Sonny Fink to the ground. Sonny shrieked as she fell backwards, with Evie jumping on top of her.

As she did so, I quickly untied Kenny, who raced to help Evie and my dad hold Fink down. There were arms and legs everywhere. Fink was screaming madly, but the trio had her secured pretty nicely with the rope she had used earlier to tie up Evie and Kenny.

'The paper, Scoop!' Evie shouted.

I turned my attention to the computer.

'Quick, Scoop,' Kenny yelled. 'Erase Fink's story and write a new story before the deadline.'

Evie gasped. 'You've got one minute, Scoop!' she said.

'Do you think that'll work?' I cried.

'It's our only chance! She said whatever is written in *The Dark Times* happens,' Kenny replied. 'Just try it!'

I could hear the wind whistling outside. If I didn't do something and fast, those gentle winds would soon morph into the deadliest storm Higgity Harbour had ever seen.

'Hurry, Scoop,' Kenny yelled. 'Hurry!'

I quickly highlighted the text and then pressed DELETE.

'Excellent! The story's disappeared!' I told them.

'Nooooo!' Fink screamed. 'You leave my paper alone!'

My brain raced. *A headline, Scoop! A headline!*

LIBRARIAN UNMASKED AS EVIL EDITOR, SONNY FINK

By Scoop Mclaren

Librarian Esther Jennings has been named as the rogue editor who has terrorised the residents of Higgity Harbour over the past two months.

The mystery of Sonny Fink's identity was solved in the basement of the town library on Thursday night.

Sergeant Mick Andrews awoke from his strange sleeping disorder to arrest Sonny Fink after *Click!*'s own Scoop McLaren and Evie Andrews, along with Ted McLaren of the *Higgity Harbour Gazette*, and his new sports journalist, Kenny Dixon, unravelled the mystery.

'Thirty seconds, Scoop,' Evie called. 'Thirty seconds!'

The group held Fink in the basement until Sergeant Andrews burst through the basement door at one minute past midnight, Friday morning.

'Don't forget Imogen,' Dad said. 'Or else she'll be stone forever!'

Higgity Harbour teenager Imogen Blaxland, who Fink had previously turned to stone, was found wandering around the library steps, safe and well.

'Ten seconds,' Evie cried. 'Hurry!'

Harmony has been restored to Higgity Harbour and residents have gone back to living their lives in peace.

'Done!' I shouted.

'Upload it,' Evie wailed above the roar of the strengthening winds. 'Upload it now!'

One press of a button… and the story was live.

Click!

CHAPTER TWELVE

Sergeant Andrews burst through the basement door at one minute past midnight. Just like I had written!

'Esther Jennings, you are under arrest on suspicion of being the criminal editor Sonny Fink,' he said, as he dragged her to her feet and handcuffed her.

'Dad!' Evie squealed. She tried to hug him as he apprehended Fink. 'I've missed you so much.'

'It's good to be back, love,' he said smiling at his daughter.

Then Imogen appeared at the door, wearing her pink polka dot pyjamas and looking utterly mystified.

'What's all this?' she asked. 'Why am I at the library?'

Evie bounced over to her and took her hand. 'Don't be scared, Imogen, everything's all right now.'

'The... the last thing I remember is sitting at my

computer in my bedroom, waiting for *The Dark Times* to arrive,' she said. 'The next thing I know, I'm wandering around the library steps, in my pyjamas!'

'Sonny Fink turned you to stone,' Evie told her.

Her eyes widened and she gasped. 'Sonny Fink did that?'

'Yes. But Scoop saved you. She promised your dad that she'd save you and she did.'

Imogen walked over and stared at me. Then she grabbed me in a hug. She smiled. 'Thanks, Scoop,' she said.

'That's all right, Imogen. I'm glad you are ok.'

'I can't believe I ever actually wanted to be like Sonny Fink. I think I'll leave the newspaper writing to you from now on.'

'Let's get Fink to the station,' Sergeant Andrews said.

'Sure thing, Dad,' Evie beamed.

'Come along, Imogen. I'll take you home to your father.'

Sergeant Andrews led Fink away, with Evie, Imogen and Kenny following behind them.

'Hey, Kenny,' I called. 'Don't forget Dad's deadlines are 3 p.m. Wednesdays and 4 p.m. Fridays.'

'Huh?'

'You're Dad's new sports journo.'

'I am?' he turned to Dad and asked.

'Well, it's written on the front page of the, I guess now, *Not-So-Dark Times*, so… it must be true!' Dad said with a smile.

Kenny grinned. 'I'll be in tomorrow,' he said. 'Thanks, Mr M… Scoop.'

♥

After they were gone, Dad and I were left in the basement. The wind had disappeared, Sonny Fink had been caught (for real this time), and all was well in Higgity Harbour again.

Dad plonked down on the floor and I plonked down next to him. We leaned against the basement wall, looking up at the ceiling. It had been a long day and I was exhausted. Solving mysteries is hard work!

'Great job there, love,' Dad said, giving me a hug. 'I can't begin to tell you how proud I am of you. There are no words. And I'm a writer!'

'Thanks, Dad. I'd like to say that I knew it was all going to work out, but for a moment there…'

'I know. I was scared, too. But you did it. How you wrote that front page in under a minute,

I'll never know. Sometimes it takes me hours just to come up with a headline that works.'

'Yeah,' I said. 'I think I surprised myself.'

'You know what the biggest prerequisite to being a successful newspaper editor is?' he asked.

'What?'

'Having a big heart' – he swung his arm around me – 'and I think you've got one of the biggest hearts in the business, Scoop. You'll also learn to trust your own instincts.'

I leaned my head on him. 'Thanks, Dad,' I replied.

Dad had actually called me *Scoop*!

♥

No issue of *Click!* was uploaded today. Instead I headed down to the football pitches for the bubble football tournament. It was so much fun! In other news, the council had to elect a new mayor to take the place of Kevin Ludwick, and now Dad's friend Tom Willis has taken over the top job. The town is in good hands with Mr Willis, Dad says.

When I got down to the football pitches Evie was there all suited up in the giant bubble we have to wear. She was giggling and rolling around all over the place. It was good to see her laughing and having fun.

Don't get me wrong, the paper is fun too, but there is also room in our lives for *fun* fun – fun you don't have to really think about. *Thanks, Kenny!*

Speaking of Kenny, he was there too, except he wasn't playing. He had his camera, notebook and pen out and was covering the bubble football tournament for my dad's page seven.

'Hey, Scoop,' he called, as I jogged up to him. 'Glad to see you could make it. Ready to get running?'

'Sure am,' I replied.

Bubble football was a blast. I couldn't remember the last time I'd laughed so much.

Evie and I lay on the grass afterwards, staring up into the perfect blue sky.

'Where do you think our next mystery will come from, Scoop?' Evie asked, rolling over onto her side.

'Who knows, Evie?' I smiled. 'But wherever it comes from, we'll be ready!'

She smiled and nodded. My roving reporter understood perfectly.

I used to think our Higgity Harbour town was boring, that nothing interesting ever happened. But the truth is that stories are everywhere and there are lots more mysteries yet to be solved. This is what a good detective editor cares about.

ACKNOWLEDGEMENTS

A big thank you to my fantastic family, especially my mum, Nita, and sister, Jane, and my wonderful friends, for all the endless support and encouragement.

To Abb McAlister, a champion human being and a real-life mayor... who has always supported me in my career and who is absolutely nothing like Mayor Ludwick!

To my kindergarten teacher, Jill Chard, who remains a good friend and a great supporter.

To American writer, the late John Hughes, whose work first inspired me to be a storyteller.

To the brilliant Beatriz Castro for bringing Scoop to life so beautifully.

And to the wonderful people at New Frontier Publishing, especially Peter and Sophia Whitfield, who took a chance on Scoop, and to my amazing editor, Stephanie Stahl, for all her hard work and for loving Scoop as much as I do.

READ ALONG FOR SCOOP McLAREN'S WRITING TIPS AND TRICKS

Hi everyone, I'm Scoop! As you know I love writing so I wanted to give you **12 tips and tricks** to get you inspired too. **Let's go!**

1. First tip, don't be afraid to ask a lot of questions on your subject. People (and especially grown-ups) usually love to talk about the thing that they are good at, so they won't mind. Also, there is no such thing as a silly question! If it helps you to understand something better, ask away.

2. Write about something you love. While I'm writing for my online newspaper, I don't have much choice but to write about whatever may be in the headlines at the time, but when I write for fun, I always choose a topic that is close to my heart. This will keep you excited to write.

3. Just write, write, write! No one expects your text to be pretty perfect right away, that's what drafts are for. The hardest part for me I find is getting started, so I just jot something down and then I work from there. It can always be changed later.

4. If you get stuck (it's called 'writer's block'), put your work away and come back to it later. Sometimes all that is needed is a little break away from your work (I like to hit the beach with Evie!) before going back to it again with fresh eyes.

5. Don't forget to do your research. Make sure you check your facts. Ask an expert on your subject, if you can. Remember, there is no such thing as a silly question!

6. Be ok when someone offers you criticism on your work. Share your work with others and take on board any advice they might like to give you to help you improve.

7. Hook your reader in with the first (intriguing!) sentence or at least the first paragraph (for a news article) because you want them to keep reading! If you're writing a story or a book, try and hook your reader on the first page.

8. Always get both sides of the story. This is very important for journalists, especially. If you only get one side of the story, readers don't see the whole picture which is super important when you have a story to tell.

9. Just like with everything else you'd like to be good at, you must practise, practise, practise. The more you write, the better you'll become.

10. Always try hard to submit your very best work. I proofread each story I've written at least three times before it's uploaded.

11. Set up a writers' group at school. It can be fun, interesting and really helpful to hang out with people who love writing as much as you do!

12. My last tip is… Read! Reading will help you become a better writer in lots of different ways. Just a few include: it improves your vocabulary (you'll learn heaps of new words!), it helps to expand your mind and it can help to inspire you to write something of your very own.

Scoop :)

Turn the page to read about
the next book in the

SCOOP McLAREN

• DETECTIVE EDITOR •
SERIES

OUT SOON

SCOOP McLAREN

· DETECTIVE EDITOR ·

BOOK 2

Feisty Detective Editor, Scoop McLaren, is back and this time the mystery has her sailing into uncharted waters!

Her childhood friend, Fletcher, is staying with Scoop and her dad over the last of the summer holidays, however strange things are happening. The peculiar events lead Scoop to suspect that someone is out to stop Fletcher from winning the harbour's most prestigious junior surfing competition.

With her roving reporter, Evie, by her side, she investigates all avenues, and as suspects are crossed off the list, one by one, Scoop is confident that she has this mystery solved.

But then Fletcher vanishes without a trace and Scoop is forced to reopen the case.

Can she track down and rescue her friend to solve this monster wave of a mystery once and for all?

ABOUT THE AUTHOR

Helen Castles graduated from Charles Sturt University with a degree in psychology and English Literature.

She divides her time between being a real-life roving reporter for a newspaper and writing about the adventures of detective editor, Scoop McLaren.

She's not fond of technology, is a nervous flyer, loves Foo Fighters music and Bill Murray films, and wants to one day live by the ocean and own a bulldog.

This is her first book series.